CAT NOEL

*A CRAZY
CAT LADY
COZY MYSTERY
CHRISTMAS
NOVELLA*

BY MOLLIE HUNT

Cat Noel, a Crazy Cat Lady Christmas Novella
(Crazy Cat Lady Cozy Mysteries #6.5)
by Mollie Hunt

ISBN-13: 978-1729516003
ISBN-10: 1729516009

Editing and Design by Rosalyn Newhouse

Published in the United States of America

Cover Art: "Nutcracker" by Leslie Cobb
©2001 *Leslie Cobb* www.lesliecobb.com

E1

Other Books by Mollie Hunt

Crazy Cat Lady Mysteries
Cats' Eyes (2013)
Copy Cats (2015)
Cat's Paw (2016)
Cat Call (2017)
Cat Café (2018)
Cosmic Cat (2019)

Short Stories
Cat's Cradle
The Dream Spinner

Other Mysteries
Placid River Runs Deep (2016)

The Cat Seasons Sci-fantasy Tetralogy
Cat Summer (2019 Fire Star Press)

Poetry
Cat Poems: For the Love of Cats (2018)

Praise for Mollie Hunt, Cat Writer:

"I know Mollie as a true, dyed-in-the-wool cat person, as a cat guardian and a foster parent and, most importantly, as a human being. One thing I can spot a mile away is true passion... and Mollie Hunt has it. People like Mollie are rare in this world because they infuse their own curiosity... with true empathy... the recipe for not only a quality person, but, in the end, a great artist as well." —Jackson Galaxy | Cat Behavior Consultant

Praise for the Crazy Cat Lady cozy mystery series:

"I knew this novel was about cats but its theme is cats! Cats are as much the main characters as the main character is! —Sharon from Goodreads

"...Each book drew me right into the story and kept me intrigued and guessing all the way. They're as cozy as can be for cat enthusiasts, but there are also some real scares..." —Catwoods Porch Party

*"...an outstanding amateur sleuth mystery that will delight cat lovers and mystery lovers alike. **Cats' Eyes** has so many exciting twists and turns; it keeps the reader fascinated until the final thrilling scene. I liked the addition of 'cat facts' at the heading of each chapter. I learned a few fascinating tidbits that I didn't know.* —Readers Favorite 5-Star Review

Praise for Cat Café:

"This book will test your observational skills and deductive reasoning... These characters have additional depth and personality." —Laura's Interests

"It's a fast-paced intriguing story. There were so many different ways it could have gone and I wasn't sure where it was heading until almost the end." —Socrates' Book Reviews

The characters are great and make this one a great read." —My Reading Journeys

Acknowledgements

A big special thank you to my long-time friend Iris Riley who walked me through some of the simpler mysteries of Wicca. Any mistakes or liberties taken were mine, not hers.

A Note about Lost Pets

If your pet becomes lost, there are many online groups that will help put the word out. Besides checking with local shelters, rescues, and vets; putting posters on utility poles; and the all-important door-to-door foot search, seek out these online sites for added assistance.

Christmas. The happiest time of the year.

The time when we come together with friends and family in one big giving, loving celebration.

The time we put our differences aside to enjoy the season.

The time we are extra specially good to one another. Peace on Earth and all that.

So why, this Christmas, was I feeling like a cat in a thunder storm?

In spite of all outward appearances, I couldn't help but sense something was amiss. The holiday lights flickered like horror show fluorescents just before the monster comes; the Christmas trees were crooked; the scent of gingerbread carried a trace of decay. *It's a Wonderful Life* was full of commercials. Someone stabbed the snowman with a candy cane. The world was running amok.

Was it just me?

Turns out it wasn't.

If you're looking for a happy, feel-good Christmas story, this isn't it. Not to say it doesn't have its merry moments—it does. And at least no one gets murdered. That's a relief, right?

It was a learning experience, and in the end... well, you'll just have to read it for yourself.

It began one week before Christmas...

Chapter 1

"...Sleigh bells ring. Are you listening?
"On the street, snow is glistening.
"La da-de-da-da, da-de-da-da..."
Rats, I thought to myself, *now I'll have that song stuck in my head all day long.*

It's not that I have anything against Christmas, not really. Aside from the commercialism, stress, expense, the social pressure... but I digress. It's just a song. A good old song. Maybe if I changed the words to something more cat-centric, I might be better able to relate:

Time to eat... Are you listening?
In the bowl, food is glistening.
Pet me pet me, pet me pet me,
Now I'm going to bite your hand...

My name is Lynley Cannon, and as you may have guessed, I am a cat person. From an early age, I was captivated by their mystical eyes, their soft fur, and their indomitable feline presence. I believe cats have a lot to add to human society; they have things to teach us if we would just curl up and listen. Now in my sixties, I happily devote much of my time to cats, volunteering at the local shelter, fostering the sick ones, and catering to the whims of my own clowder. Some think it's an obsession, but I find it more of a calling.

Today was to be dedicated to cats. I'd signed up for a morning shift at Friends of Felines, and in the afternoon, I planned to do some Christmas shopping for my kitties.

With only seven days until Christmas, I'd better get on it before it was too late.

Arriving at the shelter, I came through the big main doors to admire the pandemonium of decorations in the lobby. The large, spacious room had been transformed into a feline fairyland with twinkling lights and sparkly red and green streamers cascading from the mezzanine. A huge living fir tree stood tall beside the admittance desk, its fragrant limbs decked with photos of the shelter cats, their Cat-mas wish lists printed on the back. Under the tree lay cases of cans, bags of kibble, boxes of litter, beds, and toys galore. It made me smile to see how big-hearted people could be during the holidays. Hopefully they would remember to carry their generosity into the year ahead.

Front and center was a poster advertising the upcoming holiday fundraiser gala, the Starry Nights Fête. The artist had done a superb job of conveying the enchantment of the season with a pair of stylized kitties ballroom dancing across a field of silver-speckled indigo. As head of the fête committee, I had commissioned the poster myself and was more than happy with the results.

I spent a few minutes enjoying the friendly ambiance, then headed for the cattery. The fresh, airy space was quiet, with only a single volunteer helping an adopter choose a cat and a staff member munching a white-iced cookie at her desk in the office. After a brief hello, I set to work cleaning litter boxes for the forty-some feline residents. The rhythm of scoop, dump, scoop was almost hypnotic as I went from kennel to kennel. I even began humming a little tune.

"...Sleigh bells ring..."

Rats! I was doing it again. I sang a few bars of Monty

Python's *"Always look on the bright side of life, Da dum ba-dum ba-dum ba-dum..."* to offset the Christmas jingle.

Just as I'd disposed of the last bit of refuse and was about to take the dirty pans to be sanitized, I heard a commotion behind me. I turned to see Special Agent Connie Lee blast into the room, a frantic look on her face. She stared around, then raced to one of the unused computer stations and began to type like a squirrel.

Special Agent Lee was one of three humane investigators who worked out of Northwest Humane Society. Known to the community as animal cops, they educated the public on proper pet care and handled cases of abuse and neglect—over a thousand call-ins a year! Thankfully many of the calls came to nothing—an overly-concerned neighbor of a barking dog or a lady with what someone considered to be too many cats. But when it was the real thing, the special agents could, and did, enforce Oregon's animal cruelty laws to their fullest extent.

I'd brushed elbows with the substantial woman on several occasions, but aside from being vegan, Wiccan, and kind-natured, she was mostly an unknown to me. She had always struck me as someone who held her feelings close to the vest, yet here she was, gasping and swearing under her breath. This wasn't like her at all.

"What's up?" I asked but she ignored me, her attention riveted to the screen.

I gravitated to the counter across from her. I was hesitant to bother her yet equally as reluctant to go away and leave her in such a state. Besides, I was curious. You'd think, after all the trouble my cat-like curiosity had brought me, I'd know better. But I didn't.

Finally Connie ceased her frenzied typing and ran a hand through her short-cropped hair. She looked up, gray eyes focusing on me as if she had just then realized I was there.

"Well, this is a sad state of affairs," she announced gloomily.

"Is everything okay?"

"Not okay," she declared, her voice low and gravely. "Definitely not okay. My friend's cat is missing."

"Oh, no! Is it microchipped?"

"Yeah. I was just looking through the lost and found database, but she hasn't been recovered. Her name is Isis—like the goddess, not the terrorist group."

"How long has she been gone?" I asked, trying to call up all the helpful information one was supposed to offer on such a dreadful occasion.

"I'm not sure. A while now. I just found out about it," Connie grumbled, adding sarcastically, "My friend thought it best not to tell me, a trained humane investigator." She gave a big sigh and hung her head. "Maybe she was right. For all my training, I'm coming up with an absolute zero. Isis is still missing and I'm panicking like a newbie." Resigned, she sat back in the office chair. "I don't know what to do."

I came around and put a hand on her broad shoulder. "I'm sure you're doing everything you can, Connie. It isn't easy. Isis is probably frightened to death and hiding. When cats don't want to be found, it's really hard to find them."

"I know. I'm just scared for her. It's been raining, and now they say it's going to freeze. Isis is an indoor cat. The city's so dangerous. And besides..."

I waited for Connie to finish, but instead, she bent forward and began another rampage on the keyboard. Adjusting my glasses, I watched as screen after screen of stray cats popped up. Finally the photo of a chocolate-point Siamese filled the monitor. The banner across the bottom read: *Isis, Siamese 13 yr. 9#, Dominant color: tan, Other color: brown, Distinctive markings: face mask shaped like a heart, Lost December 10, Owner: Catherine Bremerton-Black.*

"She's beautiful," I remarked. I said the same of all cats and truly meant it, but this one was really unique. The picture had been taken in a relaxed atmosphere. The blue eyes were soft and trust-filled; the ears were straight. She had tilted her face lovingly for the camera and curved her lips in a smile. Something about Isis called to my heart, the thought of her out on her own, breaking it.

"Poor sweetie" I whispered. "But this says she's been missing for three days."

"Yeah," Connie snorted. "As I was saying, my friend neglected to tell me until today."

"Do you think something's happened to her? I mean, beyond the usual got-out-got-lost scenario?"

Connie wavered, then a look cold as steel fell across her face. "Yeah, I do."

"She is gorgeous. If someone saw her and thought she was valuable..."

"She's pretty, for sure, but there's more." Connie eyed me, as if assessing whether she could trust me with a secret. I guess she decided she could, because the next words out of her mouth were nothing I expected to hear.

"Lynley," she said carefully, lowering her voice to a whisper. "Isis is special. She's a *familiar*."

I knew Connie Lee was Wiccan but only because she'd mentioned it once or twice. I assumed she practiced some sort of get-together-with-the-goddess white magic thing, planting seeds and singing to the moon. Really I knew nothing about it except that Connie herself was one of the kindest, most compassionate, most intensely moral people I knew. Whatever her witchery might be, I never doubted it was securely on the side of the light.

I'd heard stories of witches keeping animals or birds—after all, who hasn't read Harry Potter?—but as far as real life Wiccans... "A what? You mean like magic?"

"Something like that." Connie gave a laugh but her face quickly sobered. "It's a thing, Lynley. Wiccans bond with their familiars in a very profound way. If my friend doesn't get Isis back before Winter Solstice Eve, the consequences will be dire."

"Dire? I don't understand. What happens on the solstice besides it being the longest night...?"

An explosion of static burst from Connie's radio, drowning out my question. In a microsecond, she had the instrument off her duty belt and up to her ear. "Lee here."

I couldn't make out the chatter on the other end, but in another few seconds, Connie clipped, "Copy that. On my way."

Jumping to her feet, she replaced the radio and hooked her thumbs in her belt. "Sorry, Lynley, gotta go. Hey, could you ask your cat people network to keep an eye out for Isis? Every little bit helps."

"Sure Connie, but..."

Special Agent Lee was already on her way out the door. I never got to learn about the bond between a Wiccan and her familiar, nor did I find out what part Isis was to play in the coming solstice. And as to the dire consequences that would occur if Isis wasn't returned in time, I was left to wander my own dark imagination.

Chapter 2

Christmas is for cats too. Just ask my clowder who's their Santa!

After finishing with the litter pans, rinsing them with hot water, and placing them in the sterilizer, I was more than ready for a short break. I took the elevator to the mezzanine overlooking the lobby and the glass-enclosed kitten room, and made myself a cup of tea. I chose a table where I could watch the baby cats as they chased and rolled and stalked like miniature lions. The kits were distracting, but I couldn't stop thinking about Isis. Her soft face haunted me, the sky-colored eyes set in that perfect heart of brown. All Siamese, including my own little Mab, had the tinted face mask, but I'd never seen one so uniquely formed. The result was compelling and utterly unforgettable.

Logically I knew that cats got lost all the time—many were recovered, but not all. There was something tragic about the fate of a housecat gone astray. They were so ill-equipped for life on the city streets. Pampered and fed, often living their entire lives indoors, the conundrums of a feral life eluded them. Instinct kicked in, of course, but for a cat whose biggest challenge had been catching the red dot, the stress of being lost was overwhelming and could cause lasting trauma. Some cats were never the same.

I just plain did not want Isis to be one of those unfortunates! That sweet face, so filled with love and

7

trust. I made up my mind right then and there, if I could help Isis home, I'd do it.

I finished my tea, tossed the disposable cup in the appropriate recycling bin, and went back down to the cattery. My search for Isis would have to be put on hold for a time while I fulfilled my other shelter duty: playing with cats. I belonged to a group that partnered with the behavior department helping the long-term residents keep up their spirits, and I'd planned to spend the next few hours visiting a few of those.

Muffin was the shelter's longest resident. Her standoffish nature, history of litter box issues, and the fact that she happened to be black made her go unnoticed by the public. Joule and Isotope—bonded, all-white one-year-olds—had the reverse problem. Everybody wanted the beautiful pair until they read the note on their kennel card: *Feline Leukemia Positive.* Feline Leukemia is a serious illness, and to be honest, often ends badly. It takes a special person to adopt cats with that uncertain future.

Hanging out with Muffin and the bonded pair always made me feel happy, and today was no exception. Soon enough I was so busy trying to induce shy Joule out of hiding while fending off multiple kisses from her brother I'd almost forgot Isis's plight.

Almost.

* * *

When I finished at the shelter, I headed to the Pet Pantry where I was greeted by a round woman in a bright peach-colored apron—the pet shop's gregarious owner. Harlene was short and built like a garden gnome. Her hair, which was heaped on her head in a pointed bun, added to the impression. She had a tendency to wear long, brightly colored skirts and old-fashioned blouses. With her rosy cheeks and perpetual smile, all she needed to complete the gnome persona was a red cone hat.

"What do you get for the cat who has everything?" I asked, shaking myself from gnomish fantasies. "It's that time of year again, and I'm trying to find something different for the crew."

She looked up at me with twinkling eyes. "How many kitties do you have now, Lynley?"

"Eight, only eight."

She gave a burst of laughter light as a waterfall. "Give me a rundown, then I can guide you to the perfect gift."

"Let's see," I said, doing a mental roll call. "Dirty Harry, tuxedo male. He's the oldest. Likes to eat and sleep and watch the birds out the window. Mab—she's the lilac point Siamese. She's two now and likes everything. Tinkerbelle..."

"Isn't Tinkerbelle the therapy cat?" Harlene broke in.

"That's right. We've been visiting our hospice patients like crazy. Everybody needs their kitty-fix this time of year. She could use a new toothbrush, though I'd hardly consider that a Christmas present."

"She lets you brush her teeth?"

"It's required for her visits, along with bathing and claw clipping."

Harlene erupted with another fountain of mirth. "She must be a very tolerant soul."

"Yes, she is."

"Well, bless her heart. Who else do you have?"

"Little—she's sweet and sassy. Emilio has gorgeous long black fur and knows how handsome he is. There's Big Red, my strong, shy boy, and Violet, who's even bigger than Red though unfortunately hers is all fat. She's been losing a bit on the diet the doctor set out for her—she's down to twenty pounds. And Elizabeth, the newest addition to the family. Elizabeth is a wobbly cat. She has cerebellar hypoplasia, and I'm just beginning to learn what she needs." I thought for a moment. "Did I leave anyone out?"

"Hum," Harlene considered, not finding it the least bit strange for someone to Christmas shop for their pets. "That is a diverse group. Do you want individual presents for each of them or something that will suit them all?"

As I was mulling over her question, a young man staggered out from the back room burdened with several flats of cans.

"Where do you want these, Ms. Meadows?" he puffed, his voice raspy with exertion.

"With the other cat food, Todd," Harlene answered patiently, giving me a wink.

"Oh, yeah, good idea," said the youth, as if it were a revelation.

He lurched over to the shelves clearly marked Foodies, crouched to his bony knees in the proper lifting position, and set the pile on the floor with an *oof.*

"You can put those away in a minute. I want you to come meet someone." The boy did as he was told, and Harlene winked again. "Lynley, this is my new holiday helper, Todd Tolliver. Todd, this is Mrs. Cannon. She volunteers for the shelter and has eight kitties of her own, so anything we can do to make her happy..."

The introduction was disrupted by the *brring* of the telephone. Harlene jumped as if summoned and excused herself, leaving me with the young Todd.

In fact, Todd wasn't as young as I'd first imagined, maybe mid-twenties. His head was shaved so I had no idea of his hair color—dark, gauging by his eyebrows which were thick and swarthy over deep brown eyes. His pale skin was imperfect, the flaws exacerbated by a few days' stubble and a small blue tattoo on the left side of his neck. I'd noted his lankiness as he moved around the shop, but now face to face, he seemed to shrink in on himself. His smile was self-conscious, but I put it down to being left with a stranger, a valued customer three times his age.

"Are you here for the season?" I asked to relieve the tension, "or will you be a permanent part of the Pet Pantry team?"

"I'm here through January inventory," he replied, straightening a little. "I'm hoping Ms. Meadows will be able to keep me on after that, at least part-time. I'm in my last year at Portland State." The smile was genuine now.

"Oh? What are you studying?"

"English Literature," he announced proudly.

"Sorry about that, Lynley," Harlene said, returning to the conversation. "Now let's get back to finding that perfect gift for your guys."

She gazed around thoughtfully, her face scrunched into a look of intent concentration.

"Designer food bowls? Treat puzzles? A water fountain shaped like a lotus blossom?"

None of those really struck my fancy.

"We have that new line of cat towers," Todd offered.

"That's right!" Harlene's face brightened. "They're made locally and of all natural sustainable materials. Very nice."

"You mean very expensive," I translated, "but let's take a look at them anyway. There are at least three avid tree dwellers in our clowder now."

Todd hustled back to his job, and Harlene escorted me through the aisles toward a display area at the center of the store.

"This is our top-of-the-line model," she said, doing the Vanna White up-down arm sweep more often associated with sports cars and all-inclusive trips to Hawaii.

I studied the tall, carpet-covered contraption, easily seven feet high with many perches, hideouts, and dangly things for kitty to bat while lounging. It also had steps and inclines leading to the lower levels, so even the less agile feline would have no problem making it up.

"Hum," I mused. "This would be perfect for Elizabeth, and Dirty Harry, too, with his arthritis. Violet might even be able to hoist herself onto that first perch."

"It's had good reviews for that very thing. This level..." She ran her hand along a large carpeted square with box edges about halfway to the top. "...is designed to keep a sleeping kitty from accidentally falling off."

"I can't say much for the brand name," I remarked, frowning at the laminated poster placed on the steps. "*Crazy Cat Lady* fine furnishings? Isn't that a bit stereotypical?"

Harlene laughed. "Don't take it personally. It's about the maker—she's a woman and a proud CCL."

"Really?" *Now who's stereotyping?* I chided myself, having automatically assumed the intricate structure was built by a man.

Though the high-climbing apparatus would require a full rearrangement of my living room furniture and set me back most of my Christmas budget, I decided to take it. The integrated stairs convinced me—that and the offer for the maker to deliver and set it up in my home. I suddenly wanted to meet this self-proclaimed cat lady and learn more about the workings of designing, building, and assembling such a complex device.

"How are the plans for the Friends of Felines holiday party coming along?" Harlene asked as she rung up the tree plus several other items I'd collected along the way — balls, bells, sparklies, cat catchers, and a toothbrush for Tinkerbelle.

"The fête? Good, so far." With both anticipation and anxiety, my mind touched on the preparations for the huge, end of year fundraiser. As head of the fête committee, my work had been ongoing since mid-September, but now with the event looming large, it was crunch time. "The theme this year is Starry Nights. Lots of fun opportunities for decorating. Are you going?"

"Wouldn't miss it." Harlene pointed at a calendar behind the counter. The date, December twenty-first, was circled in green highlighter.

I cringed, seeing how close the green ring was to the advancing row of red x's marking off the past. Only two more days to pull it together! But all the big stuff was finished, and the details would fall into place. I kept telling myself it was going to be fine — I was playing to a very specific audience. Though they paid top dollar for a seat at the white linen table, they were, at heart, cat people.

* * *

As I went to leave the pet store, I noticed a crowd gathering on the sidewalk in front of the door. I hesitated, assessing the group with their placards and signs, then looked back at Harlene for an explanation.

"Oh, don't mind them," she said with an exasperated frown. "They're relatively benign."

"Who are they?"

"Just protesters. They're everywhere these days, pushing their opinions on everybody, whether we want them or not."

"What are they protesting..." I began when Harlene's phone rang again. She gave a little shrug and a wave as she went to answer, leaving me to wonder what could possibly be offensive about a sweet store like the Pet Pantry.

I'd done my share of protesting back in the sixties and seventies, but that was for nuclear disarmament, the Viet Nam War, saving the whales—the big issues. Now it seemed like people made a fuss over any little thing, just to get on the six o'clock news. But I was being cynical. Many did tackle points that mattered, and there were certainly enough of those to go around.

I pushed outside, directly into a milling knot of young white men. Trying not to make eye contact, I turned toward my car but found my path blocked by a lanky picketer in a gray Columbia Sportswear jacket, black levis, and fancy Nikes with neon green soles. He hefted a big sign that read simply, *Witches Die!*

"Do you believe in Satan?" he barked into my face. His breath stunk of mint and coffee, and not in a good way.

"Um..." I didn't want to engage with the man but wasn't sure how to get around him without knocking him aside like a quarterback.

"There's evil in our midst," he went on. "You shouldn't shop here until this place is purged."

He was joined by another of his crew, also tall, also angry. His sign quoted the Bible: *Thou shalt not suffer a witch to live, Exodus 22:18.*

14

"Elvis is right," said the newcomer. "This store is in league with witches. Did you know that?"

"Oh, come on," I laughed—I couldn't help myself. "You must be joking. Harlene is one of the nicest, most non-evil persons I know."

"Not her. The other one. She's a witch, and until she gets what she deserves, we're picketing this place."

"And that's not all we're going to do!"

"Shut up, Isaac," the one called Elvis spat at his cohort as he shoved a green flyer into my hand. I glanced at the headline: *Boycott Pet Pantry! Witchcraft practiced here!*

"Well, thank you for the information." I flourished the flyer just to show I was paying attention. "Now I've really got to go."

"Mark my words." Isaac gave an ominous grin. "We're going to take care of this, one way or another."

Elvis gave him a dirty look, but added, "You're either with us or against us."

I'd had enough of this militant propaganda. I pushed in between the pair, shoving through the rest of the marchers like a tomcat on a mission. Besides not having a clue what they were talking about, I didn't like their tone, and more than that, they seemed... *dangerous* was the word that came to mind.

But I was overreacting. Just a bunch of young men blowing off steam. Still, there was a worrisome quality to their single-minded hatred.

And there was something else as well. Maybe it was the season, the proximity to the pagan celebration of the winter solstice, the annual debate on the meaning of Christmas, but it seemed an odd coincidence that this was the second time today I'd heard reference to witchcraft.

A.k.a.Wicca.

* * *

I put the protesters out of my mind and fought through the afternoon traffic toward home. Harlene had sent a message to the maker of the cat tree, Cat Black, and assured me she would be in touch soon regarding installation plans.

It didn't register at the time, but on the way home a thought nagged at me. Black—a common enough name but I'd heard it recently, if only I could recall where.

Then another thought hit, blotting out the first: *Isis, lost in the frozen city, cold and alone.* Or was it *Isis, stolen by cat thieves for some nefarious purpose?* Or could it be something even deeper and darker?

Surprised by the intensity of my concern, I figured the best way to settle it was to get going on the promise I'd made Connie to contact my cat network. The group consisted of a number of feline fans, friends, acquaintances, veterinarians, shelters, and social media sites. I'd already mentioned the plight of the missing kitty to Harlene, promising to email a photo for her bulletin board in case one of her clientele had some news.

As soon as I got my coat off and appeased my kitties with afternoon treats, I dutifully sat down at the computer. I located Isis's original listing on the lost cat database and forwarded the pretty picture of the Siamese with the heart-shaped mask to as many connections as I could think of. As I clicked the final link, I tried not to feel hopeless. After all, Isis was microchipped—someone picking her up as a stray could bring her to any vet or shelter where her family would be traced with a single swipe of their magic wand.

If, however, Isis was not lost but stolen, that would be

another matter. People were known to steal pretty pets, whether out of ignorance, greed, or just plain meanness. Breed animals were always a target for thieves who thought they could do a turnaround sale and make a few bucks.

Then there was a third possibility—that she had been cat-napped. Would there be a ransom call demanding a large sum for her safe return?

But what if it were none of those? What if, in fact, it was something even more obscure and arcane? Connie's hint that Isis's disappearance had to do with her role as a Wiccan's familiar took things in a whole different direction. Of course such a move would assume the thief knew what Isis was and with whom she belonged. Maybe they believed in whatever witchy power the cat possessed and wanted it for themselves. Or the opposite could be true—they wished for some reason to put a wrench in the works of the solstice celebrations. I thought of the protesters outside the pet store—they certainly seemed capable of mischief. Or the motive could be something else entirely. I had no way of guessing since this whole thing was beyond my realm of experience.

I was saved from my overactive brain by my phone.

"Lynley Cannon?" came a woman's voice on the line.

I didn't recognize either the voice or the number and was about to make short work of the crank call when she burst into tears. I waited for her to get herself under control, which she did in a few snorts and snuffles, then asked, "Who is this please?"

"I'm so sorry, Lynley. This is Cat Black. You bought one of my towers from Pet Pantry today. Harlene said you'd like me to come set it up in your home."

Cat Black! Suddenly it all snapped into place. "You're

not Catherine Bremerton-Black by any chance, are you?"

"That's my given name, yes, but I don't use it. Why?"

"Well, this may sound crazy, but do you have a cat, Isis, who's gone missing?"

Dead silence. Then I heard a sob and a click. Cat Black had hung up on me.

Huh? I thought to myself. *Now how am I going to get my climber installed?* But before I could sink into a really good brood, she called back.

"I'm sorry. I dropped the phone. I'm so upset. But how did you know? I've only told a few people. Harlene wasn't one of them."

"I ran into Special Agent Connie Lee at Friends of Felines. She's very upset about Isis. Apparently she had just got the news."

"Oh, Connie. Well, that makes sense then. She's mad because I didn't tell her sooner. But I just couldn't. I didn't want to believe it myself, and somehow I felt like as long as I didn't talk about it, it wasn't real. But then time went by without any word, and I had to accept the fact that Isis was gone and I needed all the help I could get. I'm devastated."

"I'm sure you are, but Special Agent Connie will do everything she can. As will I," I added.

"Thanks, Lynley. I have to have faith, right?"

I heard a sigh on the other end of the line. "But life goes on," she said, forcing an inadequate laugh. "Will you be home tomorrow afternoon for me to do your tower?"

I switched gears, trying to calculate just what it would take to clear the required sizable space in my already-cluttered living room. "I'll be gone in the morning, and I still have to move some things around before the contraption will fit. Actually I haven't quite figured that part out yet."

"I can help. I've had a lot of experience with impossible spaces. Say about two-thirty?"

"Sure, that would be great. But we can wait on it too, if you'd rather," I put in. "I'd totally understand if you need to concentrate on your cat."

"I've done everything I can," she sighed. "Work helps pass the time. It's in the goddess's hands now."

Chapter 3

Use of a pheromone spray can go a long way to making your cat feel more comfortable in strange or unnerving situations. The spray mimics the feel-good facial pheromone cats exude when they are happy and secure.

I fed the cats, microwaved a frozen eggplant parmesan dinner and brewed a cup of mint tea for myself, then clicked on the television and settled in for the night. Since darkness fell at five o'clock, eight seemed late, and by nine I was ready for bed. It had been a long day that had begun early with no indication of the strange turn it was going to take. I hadn't done anything strenuous, but the stress of the lost Isis weighed on me in a way I could never have predicted. It was as if I could hear her calling to me; the stress came from my total inability to respond.

Little and Tinkerbelle piled on the bed as I read a few pages of my book, a cozy mystery with a holiday theme to get me in the Christmas mood. It was actually working as I drifted to sleep with visions of sugarplums—whatever they are—dancing through my dreams. When morning rolled around, I had managed to put most of my Isis anxiety aside and was ready to start my day. Tinkerbelle and I were set to visit St Joseph's Memory Care Center at ten and after that, one of our hospice patients, a Vietnam veteran with end-stage COPD. Cat Black was coming in the afternoon to install my new cat tower. Would the cats love it? Would they shun it? Would they think it was a monster invading their space? Who knew with cats? Probably a little of each, but I was convinced that with time plus catnip plus a generous spritzing of pheromone spray, they would come to claim it as their own. I mean, a giant carpet-covered mountain to scratch and claw and scale and conquer, right in the middle of the living room? What's not to like?

After breakfast for all and a monitoring of the litter boxes, I checked my email. Aside from a funny video of a kitty torturing a Christmas tree, the messages either required no immediate response or were downright trash. Why had I signed up for all those political sites? Staying informed was one thing, but most just seemed to want my money — $3 at a time.

While at the computer, I thought briefly of looking up Cat Black's Facebook page to see if I could learn more about the young Wiccan, but it felt a bit like spying so I curbed my curiosity and went to locate Tinkerbelle instead.

Tink was a registered Pet Partners therapy cat, which meant she had to abide by Pet Partners rules. One of those rules set in stone stated she must go through a thorough grooming regimen before each visit. Because she's a cat and not a dog, llama, or pony, I was allowed to use a spray-on product for her bath instead of immersing her in the tub, but even so, there was always a little reluctance from the typically unflappable cat. All I could do was try to get through it as quickly as possible and move on to the good part — hanging out with people who loved her.

I packed a bag with everything we might need — cat brush, the velvet lap bed, a clean-up kit just in case — and we were on our way. The memory care center was not far from my house, but I chose to take my little red Toyota because from there we would be driving out to Gresham to visit Mike, our hospice patient. Besides, it was freezing outside, literally. I checked the porch thermometer as I left the house, and it gave me a brisk thirty-one degrees. The sky was overcast and I was sure if I turned on the radio, some weather person would be pontificating about the Big One, impending snow, and black ice. Portland had its share of ice storms, where dipping temperatures froze the ubiquitous Northwest rain into thick sheets that covered everything. It was really quite beautiful and dangerous as heck.

So far the wet pavement was still just wet and the driving was normal. Tink and I arrived at St Joseph's at exactly nine-fifty-eight, and I lugged the carrier and bag through the door to check in at the front desk.

"Hi, Lynley," said the guy behind the counter, a burly man who looked like he might be a biker in his other life. "Happy Holidays. Yvon's expecting you. Let me just call and tell her you're here."

I thanked him and gazed around at the holiday decorations which accommodated a diverse mix of tastes and cultures. In one corner hung a flock of angels; in another, the theme was elves, all decked in red and green. A silver tinsel tree stood by the fireplace, draped with gold garlands and pink satin balls. On the mantle was a brass Menorah, a Kinara of multi-colored candles, and a collection of Christmas cards from the center's many friends.

"Tinkerbelle!" said Yvon as she stepped out of the elevator. "And Lynley!" she added, almost an afterthought but I didn't mind—Tink was certainly the star of this show.

Yvon reached out and took my heavy shoulder bag from me, then led us to one of the lobby sofas. Though the twenty-something activities director with the teal-streaked hair and tattoos on every inch of her visible torso wasn't what one might expect in an eldercare home, she'd been working there for as long as Tink and I had been coming, and the residents loved her. She was energetic, optimistic, and ready for anything, a job requirement when dealing with people on the edge of oblivion. It took a special sort of mindfulness to answer the same questions into infinity, but Yvon did it with tireless grace and ease.

"I have you down for the common room, and a few personal visits with folks who are confined to their beds. Which would you like to do first?"

I considered as I opened the carrier gate and waited for Tinkerbelle to emerge—the little diva enjoyed her dramatic entrance!

"Let's do the individuals first. That way if Tink gets tired, we won't miss anyone. The commons can be stressful, depending on how many people want to see her. We usually end up going around several times."

"Sounds good. Here's the list of room numbers. See you in a while."

Yvon swished off to some other affairs, her black mini-skirt flouncing prettily over her leggings. Tinkerbelle had come out, and I hooked the leash onto her halter—another Pet Partners rule: *Cats must be held on a leash at all times.*

"Here we go, Sweetheart. Time to do your magic."

I left the carrier beside the couch tucked back out of the way, picked up the cat, and headed for the elevator. Tink enjoyed riding in my arms looking over my shoulder, the press of her warm little body reassuring us both.

I could never tell how long a visit with a dementia patient might take. Sometimes they weren't interested at all, and then Tink and I would move on to the next person, but other times they wanted to tell us their life story—twice!

The first call was with an elderly resident in the east wing. Melody wasn't bed-bound, but she refused to come out of her room. I knocked softly on the door of number fifteen. "Melody? It's Lynley and Tinkerbelle the cat."

At first I heard nothing, then a low voice called, "Come in."

The door had no lock, and Tink and I moved through the short hallway to an airy combination living-dining-bedroom. A bank of windows along one wall let in what there was of the silver-gray daylight. If I had a room like this, I thought to myself, I might not want to come out either.

Melody was sitting at her desk, a few sheets of floral stationary set out as if she'd been writing. Well into her eighties, her face was thickset and wrinkled, and her white hair swept up into a soft roll. What must have been stunning blue eyes when she was younger were now faded with wisps of cataract, but they still managed an intense, searching stare as I moved into her view.

"Hello, Melody. Here we are."

For a moment she gazed at me blankly, then her face lit.

"Tinkerbelle!" she gasped with a smile. "Oh, Tinkerbelle! Come let me see my kitty."

I dutifully brought Tink over to her. "Would you like her on your lap?"

The elderly woman nodded enthusiastically.

I put my bag on the couch, pulled out Tink's little bed,

and brought bed and cat to the woman. Placing the bed on Melody's lap, I let Tinkerbelle flow from my arms. She settled with a *purmph*, anticipating the coming pet fest.

I sat down in the antique wing chair next to the desk, keeping hold of Tink's leash, though only because it was a rule—Tink would no more run off than fly into space.

Melody petted and talked baby talk, content in the moment with the furry feline. At this point, I was extraneous, little more than a bodyguard for the princess, and I knew from experience this private cuddle could go on for a while. As my mind wandered, I looked around at Melody's things, always interested in what people kept throughout the years. The only acquiescence to the season was a tiny vintage nativity set on a bookshelf. The regular crew of Joseph, Mary, wise men, and shepherds had been joined by a Spiderman action figure, a pair of Lego guys, and a Disney-style fairy.

In a small glass-fronted cabinet was a collection of enamel butterflies, each more colorful and delicate than the last. A bookcase held books of all types and ages, from antique leather-bound tomes to yellowed pulp fiction. Sadly I doubted Melody did much reading anymore. Dementia often steals the ability to remember what one has read.

Framed art photography hung on the walls— landscapes of an Asian country, probably Japan. There were personal photos as well, from vintage black and whites to a modern color collage of a new baby. Grandson? Great-grandson? Great-*great*?

My gaze traveled along this arc of Melody's life until it came to one photo in particular, a tarnished silver frame on the bookshelf. I looked closer. It had to be Melody but a much younger version, in color but early and faded with a matte finish. It wasn't her youth that caught my attention however; it was her costume, a long white robe with an indigo symbol on the front.

"What's this, Melody?" I said before I could stop myself. I try not to ask questions of the memory-impaired since it can be frustrating for them if they can't recall, but it was too late to take it back. Besides, this seemed to be one she remembered well.

Melody laughed. "You wouldn't believe me if I told you, honey. Take a guess."

I studied the photo closer. The robe was generic enough, and I didn't recognize the flowing emblem.

"A sorority initiation maybe?"

She shook her head, grinning with her secret.

"A costume party?"

"Nope."

"Then I give up."

"I used to be a witch," she said, a gleam in her eye.

"A witch?" Wow, another witchy reference. It was déjà vu all over again!

"Yes, ma'am. Of course we didn't call ourselves that. We were just the Coven. It was a group of us gals from college."

"What did you do... this coven?"

"Oh, we'd get together in our fancy dress late at night and go out on campus or to Mt. Tabor. Once in a while we'd drive up to the Rose Test Garden in Washington Park. We'd form the sacred circle and chant, pray for peace and harmony, the good of all things. It was very positive. No spells or such."

"What school did you go to?"

"Reed College—we were Reedies." She pointed to a framed diploma on the wall, dusky with age. "I have a degree in fine art, you know."

She smiled proudly, then her face fell. "But we were talking about something—something important."

I picked up the picture and handed it to her. "About when you were a witch."

"Oh yes, surely. That was a long time ago!" she remarked with a sigh. "We'd make the sacred circle and pray for peace and harmony. It was all very positive." Melody gave a single guffaw. "We weren't supposed to take pictures. That was strictly taboo, but my friend Frances snapped this one. I've kept it all these years."

Melody paused and looked around the room as if she had just arrived there. Her gaze lit on me. "What was your name again, honey? I can't seem to hold a thought these days."

"It's Lynley." She continued to look confused. "Tinkerbelle's mom," I elaborated.

The wrinkled visage cleared and she looked down into her lap at the black cat sleeping there. "Ah, Tinkerbelle," she said softly. "Now you, I remember."

Chapter 4

The concept of an animal familiar is incorporated into many Pagan traditions. In Medieval times, familiars were considered mystical entities who would assist witches in their practice of magic. Nowadays, familiars are more commonly thought of as an animal with whom one has a magical connection.

Melody was tired and returned Tinkerbelle into my care, making me promise to bring her back soon, and the remainder of the visits were unremarkable. Tink was a hit, as usual, and we managed two more rooms and three tours around the commons where people were delighted anew each time the little feline came by. The subsequent trip to Gresham to see Mike, the combat pilot who had flown in the Vietnam War so many years ago, went nicely, and I was glad to see his health hadn't deteriorated since last we met. He was doing well in a lovely hospice house where he was respected, admired, and catered to by a company of warmhearted staff. He always told me how much he liked it there and how content he was with the prospect of it being his final home. He had no immediate plans for checking out, however, since the most recent report from his doctors said he was holding his own. He explained that just because someone is on hospice doesn't mean they're required to expire any time soon.

It was already ten after two by the time I got home, and Cat Black was due to come by at two-thirty. The first thing I did after setting Tinkerbelle free and giving her a treat for being such a good sport was to herd the rest of the clowder into the back rooms so Cat could work unimpeded by the curiosity brigade. I live alone in a sizable Old Portland house so there were two entire stories for them to occupy—in theory they should be satisfied with the loss of a single room for an hour or so, but not surprisingly, they weren't. Once I had them behind the closed door—an effort in itself—a chorus of complaints rose from the other side. In their opinion, the living room was the only place to be, and by my not allowing access, I was blatantly abusing their rights.

When Tink had finished her treat, I swept her into the back to join her brothers and sisters. Her habit after a therapy visit was to take a long nap on my bed so I doubted the banishment would be much of a sacrifice for her. The other seven were not so forgiving. Though I didn't hear much from Dirty Harry who tended to be Zen about change after sixteen years of life, I could pick out the distinct *yows* and *meows* of the others. Mab the Siamese vocalized the loudest, but I also recognized Little's distinctive trill and Emilio's base *mreow*. A periodic *mew* told me that Big Red was joining the protest though the shy boy didn't sound too sure about it. Violet weighed in with a throaty *'roww* that matched her considerable size. Elizabeth, never much of a talker, scrabbled at the door with her paws; every once in a while, I'd hear her tumble to the floor, her wobbles getting the better of her. Then a moment later she'd be right back up again. I admired her tenacity, if not her claw marks on my woodwork.

"It's only for a little while," I told them sternly through the panels. I knew they would eventually become distracted. I'd given them food and a few special treats, and sure enough, the clamor was already beginning to lapse in favor of more intriguing pastimes.

When the doorbell rang, I automatically glanced through to the Kit Kat clock on the kitchen wall: two-thirty exactly—Cat Black was nothing if not punctual. I opened the door to a blast of icy cold and a tiny, becoated woman. She was looking at the address plate, then her attention turned to me. Deciding this was the place, she shuffled inside without being asked.

"Woof!" she commented. "The temperature is dropping by the minute. I saw a few snowflakes coming down. This just might be the Big One everybody's been talking about."

I quickly closed the door behind her. We'd already had a freak snowstorm in November, but apparently that was just the beginning.

Cat was shaking herself off, shedding a long wool coat and unlooping a knitted scarf that had been wound around her neck several times. She removed fleece gloves and a little denim cap with a flower on it.

"Boots?" she asked.

I studied the diminutive girl. A few inches shorter than me which put her around the five-foot mark, she had black hair in a feathery cut that fell in a satin sheath around her face. I guessed her to be in her late twenties, though it could have been early thirties since I'm notoriously bad at telling ages. The older I got, the more everyone else just looked young. All I knew for certain was that this girl and I had more than a few decades between us.

"Boots?" she repeated. "Would you like me to remove my boots? I brought slippers." She dug in a substantial pack-type bag and retrieved a silk envelope.

"Well, yes, that would be nice." Though I preferred not to wear shoes in my house, I didn't force it on visitors, but since she came so well-equipped, I couldn't see why I shouldn't take her up on her kind offer. Besides, she would probably be more comfortable without those bulky Doc Martens weighing her down.

Cat made quick work of it, donning the pair of black ballet slippers.

"No Christmas tree?" she observed as she walked slowly into the living room where she turned a circle to take in the wall-to-wall furniture, book shelves, cabinets full of knickknacks, and the current cat climber set up in the corner. "Or don't you celebrate?"

"I do," I hemmed. "Just not yet." I'd pretty much decided not to have a tree this year since I wasn't planning to entertain, but admitting that out loud made me seem like a Grinch. "Don't worry about that. It would... will... go in the hallway."

There was a funny silence—not quite awkward but not quite easy either.

"Can I get you some tea?" I finally proposed .

"Yes, please. And then we can decide where you want to put the tower."

"Is green alright? Or I have bags if you'd like something else."

"Green's fine. Don't go to any trouble."

I started for the kitchen, then turned back.

"Bremerton-Black," I mused. "Of *the* Bremerton-Blacks? The Bremerton Hotel family?"

A strange look crossed Cat's face. I wasn't sure what it meant, but then it was gone. "Guilty."

"Wow!" I blurted. The Bremerton-Blacks owned one of the largest hotel and resort chains in the world and were millionaires many times over.

"Not wow, I'm afraid. It's a big family and my parents are third cousins once removed, as well as rather the black sheep of the clan. That's why I dropped the 'Bremerton'. I work for my living," she finished flatly.

"Oh," I said, a little disappointed today wasn't going to be the day I met my first billionaire. "Sorry."

"No problem," she shrugged. "It's a common mistake."

I continued with the tea-making, and a few minutes later returned carrying a tray with teapot and cups. Cat had seated herself on a low ottoman at the approximate center of the room, but instead of calculating a good spot for the cat tower, she was gazing out the window at the snowfall. The flakes were still few and far between. This might not be the Big One after all.

I set the tray on the coffee table and poured her a cup, hoping I hadn't offended her with my query about her heritage. She took it with a murmur of thanks and wrapped her hands around its ceramic warmth. Pouring one for myself, I sat on the couch.

I now found myself in another quandary: should I open the flood gates on the heartbreak of her lost cat or stick to business? I'm not much for business so I said, "I'm so sorry about your missing kitty."

She turned her face to me, sad green eyes filling with tears.

"I'm sure you'll find her," I added optimistically, feeling like a foolish Pollyanna the minute the words came out of my mouth.

"Yes, I am too." A tear fell, crossing a velvet cheek to drop onto the collar of her wool shirt, making a dark mark against the gray. She shivered, as if she were shaking it off.

"Now I was thinking," she began, "if we move the loveseat into the corner and that little table into your entrance hall, my tower might just fit nicely over there."

* * *

It hadn't been simple, but Cat Black handled her work with amazing strength and stamina. Not only did I have the lovely and very large cat tower installed in the living room beside a high window where the cats would have a superior outside view, but the new furniture arrangement seemed clean and friendly, and Cat had vacuumed the whole room, the hallway, and even part of the kitchen. I told her it wasn't necessary, but she had insisted, and who am I to turn down a good cleaning that didn't require my participation?

After the vacuum monster was safely put away, we had let the cats back in to discover their newly-renovated living quarters, then settled on the sofa with a second pot of tea. I was happy to note Cat Black seemed calmer now that she'd done some physical labor. She had her phone out and was talking pictures, entranced with the cats' reaction to her work. Little had already made it to the top where she nested, queen of the hill, to watch the goings-on through the window. The snow had stopped—for now.

"This is a beautiful room," Cat observed. "I don't often get to show the tower against such tall ceilings. Do you mind if I use some of these photos on my website?"

"No, please go ahead. You'll have to let me know when you post them."

"I'd be happy to." She put down the phone. "Do you have a card or something?"

Who doesn't have a business card these days? Though

mine isn't for any sort of profession, being only a picture of cat eyes on one side and my info on the other, I find it useful at times such as this.

I found the card in my purse handed it to her. She stuck it in her pocket, returning me one of her own. Printed vertically, it showed one of her multi-leveled towers. On the very center perch, sitting straight as a statue, was a Siamese with a heart-shaped mask.

"This must be Isis," I voiced.

"Yes." Cat smiled, then sobered. "I absolutely hate what she's going through."

I cringed at the thought. "I'm sorry. I shouldn't have brought it up."

"No, of course you should. I love her. I miss her. I need to talk about her. I need her to come home. Do you mind if I quickly check my email? There may be some news."

I nodded though she was already tapping away at the little phone, her photo project forgotten. She consulted the screen, then put the instrument down on the coffee table.

"Nothing yet?"

"No."

"Connie Lee mentioned..." I began slowly, "She said you had reason to believe someone could have taken Isis... on purpose. Is that true?"

Cat gave me a sharp look, but instead of answering my question, she snapped, "What else did chatty Connie say?"

"In fact," I forged ahead, hoping to draw more answers from Isis's companion than I had from the special agent, "she said it was something to do with the Winter Solstice. She told me Isis was your *familiar*." I paused, the term foreign to my tongue, "and she was to take part in a celebration." I felt relieved to get it out. Now if Cat wanted to tell me to mind my own business, it was up to her.

Instead of a reprimand, she began to laugh. "My familiar? Connie would say that. She is so into the Wicca thing."

"So it's not true?" I asked in surprise.

Cat shrugged. "It's true, I guess, sort of. I practice Wicca and am priestess to a coven, so it stands to reason my cat would be considered my familiar."

She tugged pensively at a black satin lock of hair. "My connection with Isis surpasses that of any other cat I've known. She's very smart and understands me. We go everywhere together. She likes to be with me all the time, which makes it doubly hard to think of her off somewhere alone. She misses me. She's scared—I can feel it."

Cat leaned back on the couch and closed her eyes. "I know what you're going to say. I'm letting my imagination run wild." She sat up quickly and looked me in the eyes. "But it's more than that. Really. I feel what she feels, as if it's happening to me."

I considered her for a moment: the green eyes, so imploring; the knit brow, far too young for such intense concern.

"When it comes to the power of cats," I countered, "and the power of cat people, I believe anything is possible. I've been amazed more times than I can count."

We stared at each other with a connection of our own. It seemed like she was about to say more, but then she turned away, suddenly busy with her phone again.

"But you have no idea who might have taken her?" I asked, back on the investigative track.

She hesitated a bit too long, and I knew she did.

"Tell me," I pressed. "Maybe I can help."

"Connie's right," she sighed. "I'm pretty sure it has to do with the observance of the Winter Solstice. The start of the solar year is very important to us as we honor the newborn solstice sun. It's a celebration of light marked by feasting, dancing, and devotional ceremonies. We decorate our homes with herbs and boughs and get together with family and friends to exchange presents, not unlike your Christmas. The festivities go on for several days, but Winter Solstice Eve and Day are the focus, and we have certain rituals that must be performed for the sake of the coming light."

"What sort of rituals?"

"Different covens have different traditions. Ours is simple. On the eve of the solstice, we meditate, explore the depths of our dark side. Then on the day, we rejoice in the return of the light."

"How does Isis fit in?"

"She is my guide through the dark regions. Without Isis, the journey into the shadow-self would be risky, if not perilous."

"So you think someone took her... why?"

"As priestess, I must conquer the darkness before I can lead the coven into the light."

"But what would anyone achieve by sabotaging your celebration?"

"The revels are really benign, but not everyone sees it that way. Did you know there are still some people who believe it's witchcraft, the evil, horned-devil type? They're a mixed lot really. Some are just good folks who have been misled. But some..."

She got up and walked to the window, petting Harry, who was reclining on the biggest perch of the cat tower, as she went by.

"There are some who hate paganism of any kind. In the recent past, they've been relatively innocuous, but lately they've formed an alliance and are becoming more militant. They call themselves the *Twenty-two Eighteens,* after the passage from the King James Bible, 'Thou shalt not suffer a witch to live.' Their aim is to attack anyone who practices paganism, whether it's white magic, like us, or the deepest darkest black."

"Does this have to do with those protesters outside the Pet Pantry? I assume it was you they were boycotting."

She looked up, he face white. "Yes, it's me. And I have reason to believe they are the ones who have taken Isis, taken her into the cold and gloom."

Something about the way she said it, each word a condemnation of guilt, made me shiver. "Cold and gloom? But how do you know?"

"She told me," Cat said matter-of-factly.

"Who told you? One of the protesters?"

Cat stared at me, long and hard. "That's the other thing about Isis's and my connection," she said finally, turning to the window. The light was at her back, throwing her small form into silhouette.

"It's not just feelings that we share," she said quietly. "We, meaning Isis and me... we can hear each other's thoughts."

Chapter 5

Having a special empathy with your cat is not as rare as you might think, and it's not only "crazy cat people" who report this phenomenon. It may be as subtle as cuddling on your bed when you are sick, or as extreme as warning that the house is on fire.

When I finally waved goodbye to Cat Black, I had more questions than answers. I couldn't help but wonder if she was having me on. A cat-napping anti-witch club? A long-range telepathic bond? I could accept the empathy between a cat and her human, but actual words? Places? People? Maybe she was a budding fantasy writer. Maybe it was wishful thinking—the telepathic part at least. Still, the fact remained her cat was gone. Something had happened. Who was I to discount a wild tale from a stranger I had only just met?

As she departed, Cat had asked if she could leave her van for a few minutes while she ran to the corner store to get some cranberry juice. I'd said sure before I noted the long, older-model vehicle was parked ominously close to the boundary of my neighbor's drive. Mr. Ferris was covetous of his space and had even painted a not-quite-legal yellow stripe on the curb to either side. He claimed he couldn't maneuver his Porsche in and out when parked cars encroached so closely on the ingress, and he was probably right, but I wished he didn't have to be quite so belligerent about it. There would be dark stares and grumbling if he came home to find Cat's van blocking his access, especially when the promise of ice loomed large.

I shook off my angst; after all, how long could it take to buy a bottle of juice? I began to close the door when I noticed a young, red-haired man in a long coat dragging a fat Douglas fir into the duplex across the street. Fredric Delarosa, my granddaughter's beau. Laughter tinkled from the other side of the greenery as the branches shivered and shook up the short flight of steps. I watched a little longer, and sure enough, the laugh belonged to the girl herself, Seleia Voxx.

It was both convenient and a little scary that Seleia's young man had moved in so close to me. I loved seeing more of Seleia as she dropped by on her way to or from his place, but there are things the grandmother of a newly-eighteen-year-old might not want to know. So far there hadn't been any indiscretions, no overnight stays or amorous silhouettes on the window shades. But I was eighteen once; it was only a matter of time.

"Hi, Lynley," Seleia waved overtop the tree. "Are you going to be home for a while?"

"Hi, love. Yes, are you coming by?"

"Give us a minute to get this green monster inside. See you in a few."

What a beauty Seleia has become, I thought to myself as I closed the door on the cold. In spite of being trussed up in twenty pounds of winter clothing, she was more beautiful than most movie stars. The long, amber hair cascading from her knit toque ran halfway down her back in natural waves. Even from across the street, I could see her brown eyes sparkle. And it wasn't merely outer virtue; Seleia was smart, a hard worker, and a generous soul. In fact I couldn't think of one untoward thing about her. Was it merely a case of grandmotherly pride? No, not at all.

I went to clear the tea things and shoot another admiring glance at my new cat tower. There were five cats on it now: Little, still claiming the high vantage, had been joined by Tinkerbelle, and the two black cats were cozied up together on the carpeted shelf; Harry was sacked out on the big perch; Mab had taken the next level down, batting at a ball on a string that hung tantalizingly within reach. I was elated to see Elizabeth curled contentedly in the mid-way basket. Though I probably would have fainted had I watched her navigate the steps with her wobble, the fact that she'd made it was an achievement in itself.

The little CH cat was a handful, both because she was young—only a bit over one, the vet had assessed—and because of her condition. Cerebellar Hypoplasia was the result of the cerebellum not maturing properly before the kitten was born, causing her to have trouble with movement. Symptoms varied from mild to extreme, and Elizabeth's case was somewhere in the middle. I'd already started her on a regimen of exercises to strengthen her muscles which would help compensate for the wobble factor. Climbing into the basket on her own proved it was working.

As I dumped the spent contents of the tea ball into the compost, I considered making another pot for Seleia but decided to put together a pitcher of hot spiced cider instead. The almost-snow-day cried for apples and cinnamon. I speculated whether Fredric might be joining her as he often did. Fredric, another hard worker, was always welcome and I was happy of his company. Both he and his aunt Grace were employed in Portland's budding film industry, and his stories from the set were always intriguing. The fact he never failed to ask if there was anything I needed doing around the house was reassuring for a single senior woman. I paid him for his labor, whether it was hauling, yard work, or maintenance, but I got the impression he would as happily—or almost as happily—have done it for free.

I heard the door open and shut just as I put the lid on the cider pot.

"We're here, Lynley," Seleia called, "and we have a surprise for you."

"Come on in, I'm in the kitchen."

"I think you might want to come out here," Seleia giggled.

I wiped my hands on a tea towel and started toward them, then stopped in my tracks. The twin of the Doug fir I'd seen going into Fredric's was now standing in my living room, propped up by a tall, hazel-eyed elf. I had to admit the costume was very becoming on him, his dark carrot hair curling rakishly from beneath the feathered cap. One thing about Fredric having grown up in theater: he didn't have a modest bone in his body.

"We got you a tree," Seleia announced somewhat redundantly.

I came into the room and inspected the gift. "For me?"

Fredric and Seleia both nodded enthusiastically.

"Oh, Grandmother, do you like it?" Seleia gushed. "It's my first real tree! Mother always has the fake white one, to go with her minimalist decor. Isn't it beautiful? And it smells so good!"

"It's lovely," I freely admitted.

"We were afraid you might already have one," Fredric said, "but figured we could always give it away if you did." He gazed around at my plain, untrimmed rooms.

41

"Looks like we made it in time though."

"Yup," I gulped, refraining from mentioning I'd been about to pass on the entire thing.

"Mmmm, I smell cinnamon," Seleia purred.

"I made spiced cider. Would you like some?"

"Yes, please. We can drink it while we decorate the tree. Do you have any Christmas music?"

I laughed. "I really rather doubt it."

"That's okay. I've got a CD in my car," Fredric volunteered. "I'll get it while I grab the tree base and clippers. Don't worry, Lynley. We weren't going to leave you to wrangle this bush all by yourself."

"And I'll fetch the decorations," said Seleia. "Are they still in the attic?"

"Yes. Make sure none of the cats follow you," I cautioned. "They're so curious about the attic, and you know how hard it is to get them out again."

As Fredric ran off to his car and Seleia went upstairs to retrieve the boxes of balls, bells, and vintage cat ornaments packed away in their Rubbermaid totes, I poured us all big mugs of cider. This was so unexpected. I thought back to when Seleia was a little girl, how I'd let her trim my tree in whatever fashion she chose. Of course I'd have to come back and finish it after she left since she could only reach partway. She had a good eye, even as a child. I couldn't wait to see what she would do now.

Fredric made a bounding return, arms laden. Dropping the base by the tree, he popped the CD into the player, raised the clippers high, and proclaimed in an elfin trill, "Let's get jolly!"

* * *

"Gorgeous!" I remarked.

"Beautiful!" agreed Seleia.

"A wonder to behold," Fredric said in elf-speak which was basically a bold British accent in a high tone of voice. He'd been employing the affectation throughout the afternoon. Rehearsing, he called it, though he denied having any upcoming roles, and to my knowledge his world in film was centered entirely off set.

His sentiment was spot-on though, as they would say across the pond: the tree was a wonder. Since the new cat tower had claimed the extra space in the living room, we'd set it up in the entrance hall framed by the wide pocket doors like a Christmas card. As the three of us lounged with our ciders, admiring its glory, we congratulated ourselves on a job well done.

Seleia had insisted on using every single cat ornament I owned, which counted above fifty, along with several boxes of clear globes, shiny red balls, and many yards of antique bead garlands. Fredric had rigged the lights, both tiny white ones that sparkled like snowflakes and fat, colored ones, the type that was popular in the 1950s. On top of that was a tasteful sprinkling of tinsel. For those of us who hold the philosophy that more-is-better-at-Christmastime, it was perfect.

The sun had long-since set, and the tree lit the room with a magical glow reserved solely for the holidays. The cider jug was empty and so was the plate of red- and green-iced cookies Seleia had brought with her from the bakery where she worked.

"Now all I have to do is keep the cats out of it," I said with a sigh.

"Maybe you need one of those dog fences to put around it," Seleia suggested.

"We should have hung it from the ceiling," said

Fredric, "like the one on the internet."

I'd seen that picture too. More than one friend had posted it to me—just part of being a cat lady, I suppose.

"I've been lucky in the past," I said. "My cats don't really go for the tree. They have other things to amuse them."

"And we didn't hang anything breakable on the lowest branches," Seleia commented, "in case they try."

"I'll keep an eye on them, and since we put it in the hallway, at night I can close the pocket doors."

"That new cat tower ought to keep them busy," said Seleia, turning her attention to Emilio, Mab, Violet, and Dirty Harry who were currently claiming various perches. "What do you think? Should I get one for Solo?"

I felt a pang of melancholy. Up until recently, Solo had been my cat. She'd always been shy of people, but then suddenly she became more reclusive than ever. A cat behaviorist proposed she might be better off in a home without so many other cats. Seleia, who had formed a bond with Solo, had begged to take her, so after much deliberation, Solo made the big move. It was working— according to Seleia, Solo no longer spent all her time under the couch, so mission accomplished—but I still felt a little like a failed cat mom.

"She's doing really well," Seleia was saying. "She only goes under the couch if someone comes over or if there is a loud noise. She sleeps on my bed. Oh, Lynley, I'm so blessed to have her!"

Seleia jumped up and gave me a little hug. How could I feel sad about this perfect solution?

"I'm sure Solo would benefit from a climber," I considered. "Maybe not such a huge one, but they come in all shapes and sizes. This one was made by a local woman,

Cat Black. She gave me her card if you want to call her."

Seleia already had her phone out and was tapping away. "Cat Black?" she repeated. "Here's her website. Ooh, just look at all the beautiful designs." Seleia scrolled down, then held it out for me to see. "Mother might like this one. It's simple and elegant."

I looked at the style she picked, an all-white slim-lined model about five feet high. Its three perches were padded with white upholstery-grade velvet. "That might work. I'd ask Lisa before you order though. She might have other thoughts."

I gave an inadvertent twitch as I thought of my daughter Lisa. The woman had exacting tastes, whether it be food, environment, or decor. She'd always been that way, and I'd teased her when she was a kid that she was as finicky as any of our felines. Though a pain in the patootie to buy gifts for, there was no denying Lisa's impeccable style. She was, after all, an artist, and a good one. Just because her strict monochromatic minimalism wasn't my thing didn't mean it was wrong.

Seleia was still studying her phone. She had stopped her perusal and seemed to be reading.

"Hey, Lynley," she said after a minute. "Did you know Cat Black is a high priestess? If it's the same one, that is."

A stab of cold doubt ran through me. "Here, let's see."

She passed over the phone, a photo of a small woman in a white robe holding a candle. Though her eyes were covered by a cat-face mask, it was Cat Black for sure. I read the headline: *Paganism—Home for the Holidays?* It was dated a little over a week ago.

I was just starting to read when Frank Sinatra's "White Christmas" burst from the instrument and a number flashed across the top of the screen. With a quick apology,

Seleia grabbed it to answer the call. I would have to finish the Cat Black article later.

"Sorry, Lynley," Seleia said as she hung up. "I've got to go. Lisa is having people to dinner, and my presence is required."

"Oh, well, you can't keep your mother waiting."

I tried not to let my exasperation show. The fact that Lisa and I didn't have the best mother-daughter relationship wasn't totally Lisa's fault, and it had nothing whatsoever to do with Seleia. Since my daughter had grown up and come into her own mind, there had been a personality clash. She disapproved of everything I did, from my cluttered and untidy housekeeping to my overt love of cats. She probably had a point about the house, but it's hard to face condemnation without instinctively lashing back. Things had got better in recent years, but we still had a way to go. *Someday*, I promised myself, *we might yet work it out.*

"Well, I guess that's my cue," Fredric said, leaping to his feet. "Is there anything you need doing while I'm here, Lynley?"

"I'm good right now," I told him with a smile. "But be sure to take your clippers with you. Thanks for setting up the tree."

The young man doffed his elf cap and gave a deep bow. "T'was nothing, Madam. And thank ye for the draught."

Seleia was rustling into her coat, hat, gloves, and scarf. She gave me a big, padded hug. "That was really fun, Grandmother. I'm sorry I have to run off. But we'll see you on Christmas, right?"

I gave my best noncommittal grin, but let the answer hang. This year Lisa was organizing a huge event with all

46

her many eminent acquaintances from far and wide. It would be hours of stilted, blasé conversation in a near-sterile atmosphere; well-heeled people in designer clothing and tissue-paper hats—hardly my cup of tea. I tried not to think of it as an ordeal, an unwanted performance with one aim: to say the right things, try not to offend anyone, and get out as fast as politely possible.

As Seleia and Fredric hurried into the night, on to their other destinies, I noticed three things:

The streetlights had come on, and even though it couldn't be much more than six o'clock, it was dark as midnight.

The sky was sprinkling tiny single snowflakes that if put under a microscope would show as perfect mandalas.

Cat Black's van remained stolidly parked at the lip of my neighbor's driveway.

Chapter 6

When your sweet kitty rubs her sideburns on you, she's doing more than just saying hello. Cats have facial pheromones, chemicals that are perceived as scents, that they use to indicate people, places, and things as safe and friendly. Essentially Kitty is marking you as her own.

I stepped back inside my house, closed the door, and headed to the kitchen for a quick supper, admiring the twinkling tree and the new cat tower as I went by. It had been a momentous day all around, and it wasn't over yet. In another hour, I planned to meet up with a few folks from Friends of Felines to go caroling in Peacock Lane. Luckily for me the lane, Portland's famed "Christmas Street," was only a few blocks away. I didn't even need to take the car.

As I flicked on the kitchen light, the stark brilliance instantly vanquished the homey holiday ambiance. Fredric's Christmas music, a classic hymn, had chosen that moment to cut off, and like waking from a dream, I was back to the reality I knew. No adornments here—just a note on the cork board to get toilet paper and molasses. Okay, the molasses was for gingerbread, at least a tiny bit Christmassy.

I opened the fridge and checked for leftovers—a few shreds of bright orange grilled squash and some salad. I added a handful of green beans which I would steam, and a dollop of quinoa, some oil and vinegar dressing, and a sprinkle of lentil sprouts I'd learned to grow myself. Ever since I'd partnered with outspoken vegan Esmae Westhouse selling cat costumes at Bridgetown comic-con a few months ago, I'd had a greater appreciation for vegetarian food. Many animal advocates refuse to eat or use any animal products whatsoever. I doubted I'd be getting rid of my leather sandals any time soon, but skipping cow, pig, or fowl in my daily meals didn't seem much of a hardship.

Topping off the vegetable plate with a few grapefruit sections and a fat strawberry that had undoubtedly traveled farther than I ever would, I sat down at the table and dug in. The cats, tired out from their afternoon adventures, were napping and thankfully left me alone.

With no cats to demand attention, no TV to watch, no music to listen to, my mind wandered.

What could I get Lisa for Christmas that she might want but didn't already have?

Would there be a last-minute snafu with the FOF Starry Nights fête?

What was the deal with Cat Black?

That last one eclipsed all else. Pulling out my phone and bringing up the internet, I searched for the article Seleia had shown me. It didn't take much to find it, and I congratulated myself on plugging in the correct keywords: Cat+Black+Paganism. Okay, so maybe it didn't take a rocket scientist, but I can remember back in the olden days when we had to saddle our horses and mosey on down to the library for such information.

The article had been published in one of Portland's more obscure underground newspapers and wasn't very long, more of a fluff piece by a freelance journalist looking for a buck. In spite of the provocative headline, the article itself was mostly a thin comparison between Christian Christmas and the pagan celebration of the Winter Solstice. Nothing I hadn't heard before and little more on Cat Black besides the photo caption. Well, at least now I knew what she looked like in costume.

I peered at her fancy dress, then enlarged the picture so I could see more clearly. It was the requisite long white robe, but what was that on the front? Adjusting my glasses, I made out a dark symbol very much like the one on old Melody's dress from long ago. It must mean something, but I had no idea what. Maybe I could ask Melody—she seemed to recall that part of her past well enough.

How deeply had the old woman delved into the pagan arts? I wondered suddenly. *Had she, too, kept a familiar?*

Again I thought how terrible as it was for someone to lose their pet, and it seemed that the case of a witch losing her familiar must be even more tragic. Though one automatically thought of a witch's companion as a black cat, according to Harry Potter, it could be a number of animals, from owl to bird to toad. The common thread was the innate bond they shared with their person.

Whether I bought the idea that Cat Black's cat had been filched by anti-paganists or someone else with an unknown agenda, one question remained: How had they pulled it off? Doubtful Cat let Isis roam the open streets for anyone to nab and grab. On the other hand, if someone had deliberately broken into Cat's home, then darker motives began to take shape.

I personally had no problem with other people's beliefs, as long as they caused no harm, but I knew from hard experience not everyone was so tolerant. Could someone have a grudge against Wiccans, a grudge worth breaking the law? That was what Cat believed. But here the scheme fell apart. Granted Cat, according to the newspaper article, was the high priestess of her coven, and granted Isis was a necessary part of their Winter Solstice ritual, but if things didn't go ahead as planned, what difference would it make in the long run? There must be hundreds of covens all over the world, dozens in our area alone—disrupting one of them would be terrifying for Cat and Isis, but in the grand scheme of things, it wouldn't make the slightest ripple in pagan practice.

For a moment I considered a bigger conspiracy, with anti-paganist groups stealing familiars all over the land. But that was silly and paranoid. Besides, wouldn't Cat have heard through the coven grapevine and at least mentioned that Isis wasn't the only one gone?

Which brought me around again to the more likely prospect: Isis was lost and not stolen at all. Perhaps the cat had accidentally got outside. Even the best intentions to keep kitty indoors can go awry if kitty has other plans. But Cat had vehemently discounted that idea, and I tended to accept her instinct.

Once I ruled out accidental loss, kidnapping, and an anti-paganist plot, another notion began to form. What if it were a more personal motive, something to do with Cat Black, herself? How better to hurt or scare someone than to filch their beloved kitty? I knew I would do almost anything to save one of my clowder and was absolutely certain Cat felt the same way.

The Kit-Kat clock chimed the half hour. Where had the time gone? I was due to meet the carolers in twenty minutes. I needed to quit obsessing on things beyond my control and find my mittens.

I still wasn't sure why it tormented me so. I suppose it was the thought if the poor cat in an unknown situation. Cats hate change at the best of times, and being carted away by a stranger was edging close to the worst. I had no reason to think they would do Isis harm, but considering all the crazies the world, I couldn't rule it out either.

I picked up my bowl and put it in the dishwasher, pushing my helplessness aside. There was nothing I could do beyond hope for a quick return and maybe throw in a heartfelt prayer or two.

A sleepy Little wandered in and rubbed her cheek against my ankle, claiming me. I reached down and petted her gently, adding a second prayer that nothing like this ever happened to one of my own.

* * *

The feel of the snow falling softly on my face was more exhilarating than chilling, but underneath the thin film of white was a sheet of pure ice. My walk down to Peacock Lane had been slippery to the point of precarious, but with the help of a pair of thick wool socks overtop my boots, a technique I'd learned in the wilds of Canada, I'd made it unscathed. Not everyone had fared so well however, and I passed an ambulance picking up a downed woman on the other side of the street. I'd suffered these ice storms before and knew what to expect, but others were not so prepared.

As I waited on the corner of Belmont and Peacock Lane, I took deep breaths and tried to clear my mind of anything aside from the colorfully-lit houses and the multitudes of people enjoying their night out. The lane itself was a four-block row of quaint Tudor homes that, though unremarkable for most of the year, burst into full holiday bloom at Christmastime. Since 1929, people had been coming from miles around to marvel in its brilliance and spirit, and this year was no exception. In spite of the black ice warning, there was a good crowd strolling up and down ogling the displays—everything from a full-sized classic nativity scene to a huge inflatable Darth Vader with reindeer horns.

I felt a touch on my shoulder and turned to find Frannie Desoto smiling through puffs of frozen breath. I automatically broke into a smile. I considered the fellow Friends of Felines volunteer to be my best friend, and we often enjoyed spending time together having lunch, taking cat classes, and going on excursions such as this caroling caper. Though we were roughly the same age, Frannie's consummate use of makeup and dress gave the impression she was quite a bit younger. Tonight, decked out in a fuzzy leopard print coat, purple mittens, and a brown knit cap with cat ears, she looked young at heart as well. Lipstick and eyeshadow matched the purple mitts, as did her shiny boots. Sometimes I envied her fashion style—something I had little of—but mostly I admired the way she could pull off any costume and make it look like a million bucks.

"Brrr," I said, giving her a greeting hug. "The weather could have been warmer. I hope my voice doesn't freeze up."

"But this is perfect!" she remarked, stomping her feet in the snow. "Isn't this what everyone wants for the holidays? It's like being inside a snow globe."

I looked skeptically at the swirling flakes. "It's pretty, but I could do without the black ice."

"Still not feeling it?" she asked, knowing I went

through a certain amount of angst every year at this time.

"No, not really. Well, maybe a little. Seleia and her beau came by this afternoon with a tree for me. We decorated it and listened to Christmas music. That felt pretty holiday-ish."

"There you go, Lynley." Frannie patted my arm with a soft mitten. "You'll get there. You always do."

I nodded and sighed. She was right. I may be a slow starter, but when Christmas rolls around, I am usually able to put my Grinch-face aside. Still, I wasn't so sure about this year. Scary things were happening in the world; how could anyone feel entirely safe?

And scary things were happening closer to home. "A friend's cat is missing," I said bluntly.

I had no doubt that Frannie, also a dedicated cat person, would immediately understand the implications, and she did.

"Oh, no!" she exclaimed. "And now the cold weather. No wonder you're not enthusiastic about the snow."

"Her human thinks it might be a cat-napping."

Frannie stepped back and peered at me.

I removed my glasses and polished off the flakes with my scarf. "It's a long story," I conceded, "and I don't really know the girl that well. Or at all," I finished off.

"Sounds like you've found yourself another of your conundrums, Lynley. Do you want to talk about it?"

"Yes, but not now," I said as I spied two ladies carefully picking their way over from the parking lot across the street. They waved and I waved back. "After caroling?"

"Hot chocolate at Zeno's?" asked Frannie as we were joined by the others of our quartet.

"It's a date."

Chapter 7

How cute is that? Your kitty stares excitedly at the new sparkly thing in the room—your Christmas tree. But unfortunately Christmas trees hold many dangers for cats. Tinsel and other decorations may be hazardous if ingested. That ball kitty knocked off and broke is made of glass and can cut. Your cat may be tempted to climb the tree and get hurt if it falls. You don't have to give up your tree, but be aware and careful.

Frannie and I scooched into Zeno's bright red plastic seats. By some miracle, we had found a small booth at the popular chocolatier, and I, for one, was ready to settle in for the duration. Though we hadn't been caroling all that long—maybe forty-five minutes at most—the chill had seeped through all my layers of clothing, and by the last few strains of Good King Wenceslas, my teeth were chattering. It created a sort of vibrato to my voice which was not altogether unpleasant, though I wouldn't recommend freezing one's buns off to achieve the effect.

"I should have worn a heavier coat," I said, scrutinizing my thin fleece jacket as I shed it in the cozy warmth of the café. "I always forget how cold snow actually is."

"We don't get that much freezing weather here." Frannie pulled off her faux fur, shook out the residual flakes, and hung it over the seat next to her. "At least we didn't used to. It seems like the past few winters have been worse than usual."

"Global warming?" I joked.

"You mean *climate change*," she corrected in all earnestness. "It's not just warming, Lynley—it's about changing climate patterns. I just saw a new documentary on PBS. Did you know that the average global temperatures have increased markedly since the industrial revolution in the early eighteen-hundreds, and they show no sign of slowing down?"

"Like I said, global warming."

She gave me a dirty look. "They used to call it that, but it gave the wrong impression so they updated the term. It's not just about heat and drought—climate change is responsible for all sorts of weird weather from floods to hurricanes to snowstorms. It's causing extreme conditions all over the world. You should know that, Lynley."

"I..." I began.

She held up a hand and clicked off on her purple-tipped fingers: "Heat waves in India; the East African drought; South Asia floods; freezing temperatures in Florida; snow in Texas."

"Right now, I'm only concerned with the snow right here in Portland, Oregon," I commented, looking outside at the icy landscape. "Frannie, I do know about climate change—who doesn't? I was messing with you."

"Oh," she said with a deflating groan. "Of course. I should have guessed."

A waitress appeared, decked out to Zeno's nineteen-fifties specifications in a red dress, white bibbed apron, and petite red-and-white checked hat. Though probably still in her early twenties, she had taken the time to do her hair in a vintage French twist. Maybe it was required, though the other girls on the floor seemed to be content with ponytails.

"You ladies decide what you want?"

"Two hot chocolates please," I said.

"Marshmallows or whipping cream?"

I looked at Frannie and she at me. "Both," we said in unison, then giggled. The girl gave us a knowing wink as she rushed off. Apparently we weren't the only folks to indulge in Zeno's famous extras.

"Now tell me what's up with the missing kitty," Frannie said as soon as we were alone. "What's your connection?"

I quickly outlined my run-in with Special Agent Connie Lee at the shelter and her saga of the missing Isis; my trip to the Pet Pantry and the purchase of the climbing tower that coincidentally was made by Isis's cohabitor, Cat Black; the article in the underground paper naming Cat as a high priestess of a Wiccan coven; the anti-witch protesters, and Cat's own theory that Isis was stolen by the Twenty-two Eighteens. Our drinks came just as I'd finished, and for a while we were sidetracked by the hot, sweet, steaming chocolate concoctions.

"It sounds terrible," said Frannie, wiping the brown-tinted whipped froth from her lips, "but I still don't get your involvement. It's Miss Black's cat, and Special Agent Lee is already looking into it. I know it's heartbreaking to think of our kitties beyond our safety net, but honestly, Lynley, what can you do? Are you sure you're not using this as an excuse to ignore other things, such as getting ready for Christmas?"

"I'm working on that," I bristled.

"Lynley sweetie," she said, placing her hand on mine. "I mean no disparagement. It's just that, what with planning the FOF fête as well as the usual holiday extras—

57

buying gifts, decorating, contacting old friends, baking..."

"You know I don't bake."

"That's not true. You told me you were going to make gingerbread cats for the volunteer party."

"Yes, but they don't have to be good as long as they're cute and I don't burn them."

"All I'm saying is that this time of year can slam you. You've got enough on your plate as it is. Why worry over something you can do absolutely nothing about?"

I was ready to give some curt retort when I realized she had a point. I'd wondered about it myself. Why did my mind keep circling back to the case of the missing Isis when it really had nothing to do with me?

I took a sip of cocoa, letting the satin warmth curl around my tongue, soothing my rampant mind. "You're right, Frannie. You're absolutely right. And I don't have a good answer for you. I guess I'm just worried about her. You know how it is."

"Yes, I do." Frannie settled back in her seat. "And I know you want to help all cats everywhere on earth, but you have to think about yourself. You have cats of your own to worry about, and cats at FOF as well. Unless this Cat Black actually comes to you for help, I suggest you forget about it."

"And how am I supposed to do that?"

Frannie smiled. "You are the master of your brain," she said with a knowing wink.

* * *

After we bought an assortment of hand-made truffles from Zeno's showcase selection—milk chocolate for Frannie and dark for me—Frannie gave me a ride back to my house where we parted, planning to see each other the next day at the Bremerton Inn where we would be putting up decorations for the fête. I couldn't believe tomorrow was the big night, but as Frannie said, I was (theoretically) the master of my brain, so I quit worrying... for the moment. The morning would come soon enough, and then I could run around like a kitten chasing her tail dealing with the last-minute issues.

All the way home I had my fingers crossed that Cat's van would be gone. Crossing one's fingers, by the way, is a plea to benign spirits for luck that dates back to pre-Christian times—dare I say pagan? But those spirits didn't seem to be listening. The vehicle was still parked in all its funky glory. A dusting of snow had accumulated on the windshield. No one had approached, no footprints tracked anywhere near. Where was that girl?

I bid goodnight to Frannie and watched her taillights disappear down the street. Even though the ground was barely white, it was slick with ice, and I gritted my teeth as she fishtailed to a stop at the corner. The main roads were still passable, but these side streets were already turning ugly. What would we wake up to in the morning? Would we even make it to the Inn when just walking to the car risked life and limb?

Portlanders didn't do well with snow and ice. Most refused to leave their homes once the first flakes had fallen, and the rest, the brave and oblivious ones, had no clue how to manage in it. Snow was bad enough—people drove like the white stuff was just so much confetti and then were surprised they couldn't stop when they braked—but black ice was even worse. There would be pileups and spin-outs. Even those who did know how to drive on the glass-like slick were at the mercy of those who didn't.

Portland had been the victim of some terrible ice storms in the past. I remembered back in seventy-eight when the city was brought to a standstill for an entire week. I'd holed up with my parents who were both still alive then and in a much better living situation than me. When the wires came down under icicle weight, we huddled around the fireplace. After the initial deluge, the sun came out, blazing off the hillocks of glossy white. The sky was an unending azure, while trees, leaves, berries, and branches down to the tiniest twig were encased with a good half-inch of crystal. It was a magical wonderland, and once its hardships had passed, a fond memory.

But I digress. Even as I watched, my neighbor Mr. Ferris pulled up to his driveway, eyed the van, saw me on the sidewalk, and rolled down his window.

"This was here when I left," he accused.

I inched a little closer to my gate, ready to make a run for it if he got on one of his parking police rampages. "It belongs to a business associate of mine. She left it while she walked up to the store. She should be back any time."

Mr. Ferris frowned. "Well, I suppose I can pilot around it, but pulling out again is another matter, especially with this ice. Besides, if this is the Big One, I don't want her stuck there." The window slid closed, and with the spinning of heavy tires, he eased into the drive, making a big deal of crawling forward and back until he got the car lined up just right. Then, clicking open his automatic garage door, he zipped in, kicking up snow in his wake.

I was glad to get Mr. Ferris off my back, but I felt bad for fudging the truth. Cat had been gone to the store for some hours now. If she had been distracted or diverted, she really should have let me know.

What if something else had detained her? I thought with sudden apprehension. *What if something had happened to her? Could Cat Black, like Isis, have gone missing too?*

None of this felt right to me. I didn't know much about the girl, but I'd liked her. Still, she was of the age and artistic temperament that could account for any number of reasons why she hadn't returned aside from my speculation she had been wickedly waylaid. She could have met a friend as she walked by the Pub and Pony. She could have decided, with the snowfall, to hop a bus back home instead of risking the drive. Creative inspiration could have struck, moving her in all sorts of directions. I might be well past my spontaneous youth, but she wasn't.

I shuffled through the gate, making the first black footprints on the blue-white of the walkway. The steps were slick with ice—I needed to have them retextured. Maybe Fredric could do it this spring. Once inside my house, I threw off my winterwear. Relishing the warmth, I clicked on the Christmas tree lights, briefly admiring the beautiful boughs that thankfully seemed untouched by little paws. Then I dug out my phone and located Cat's business card with her number on it. It couldn't hurt to give her a call.

Big Red meowed up at me balefully as I let the number ring. After what seemed like an inordinately long pause, a monotone voice came on the line:

The mailbox is full and cannot accept any messages at this time. Goodbye.

61

Chapter 8

Most animal shelters survive on volunteer help and donation dollars. As the saying goes: "ADOPT, but if you can't adopt, FOSTER. If you can't foster, VOLUNTEER. If you can't volunteer, DONATE. If you can't donate, SHARE and EDUCATE. Everyone can do something to help save a life."

I woke the next morning to the usual chorus of meows and slipped on my glasses to check the time. Seven-fifteen, though it felt much earlier. I hadn't slept well, having mixed-up dreams about an ice cavern full of cats, and when I went in to save them from the monster, Cat Black was there, decked out in full witch regalia. I looked around for Isis, but she was nowhere to be seen.

Where's Isis? I asked. Cat reached up and pulled off her mask, revealing not her pretty eyes and cute haircut but a dark black void. Without a voice, I heard her say, *She is where she is.*

Ugh. I sat up and shook it off. It hadn't been truly scary, not like an all-out cold-sweat scream-in-the-dark nightmare, but there was definitely a disturbing element to it. What did that mean—*She is where she is?*

But it was a dream. It didn't have to mean anything at all, other than I'd been thinking too much when I went to bed, and the pepperoncini sandwich I'd eaten before bedtime probably hadn't helped the matter.

Sliding on my robe and scrunching my feet into cat-print slippers, I made for the kitchen, site of all good morning things such as coffee for me and cat food for everyone else. I went through the complex ritual of feeding eight cats with different diets and making a big cup of steaming coffee from the Keurig, but my mind wasn't on the job. When I opened the curtains, I was happy to see it hadn't snowed much more overnight. I was not so happy to see Cat's van still parked across the street.

After being unable to reach Cat the night before, I'd called Special Agent Connie. She assured me she would look into the girl's disappearance and get back to me as soon as possible. Maybe seven in the morning was pushing it, but shouldn't she have texted by now if she'd had word?

Another possibility came to mind—Cat Black was still in the wind.

* * *

When I arrived at the Bremerton Inn conference center only a smattering of cars dotted the parking lot. The driving had been a bit hairy, what with black ice still menacing the intersections and side streets, but it wasn't as bad as I'd feared. The lot itself could have doubled as a skating rink, but a portion had been salted, and I grabbed a spot near the front door.

It was still early, nine-ish, and for a moment, I sat in my warm car-cocoon gazing out at the expanse of flawless pearl. Deciduous trees lined the perimeter, their black branches perfectly outlined in white. Cracking the window, I felt the cool air rush in, uncharacteristically clear. What happens to the smog when the temperature dips? Does it fall to the ground, frozen too?

I had left my car radio off during the drive, not wanting to risk another holiday earworm. Besides, so much of what they played is not to my taste. When it comes to Christmas music, I'm strictly a classics girl—"Joy to the World" and bits from the "Messiah," with a sprinkling of forties and fifties holiday pop thrown in. Though I do enjoy hip hop, a rap star's rendition of "Santa Baby" doesn't move me. I suppose I could have brought Fredric's holiday CD, but honestly, I still wasn't feeling it. Maybe after the fête was over; maybe when I wasn't so busy...

A bronze vintage Volkswagen Beetle pulled into the space beside me, and two women got out: Frannie and another Friends of Felines volunteer, Alani. Alani was a round-faced, round-bodied woman with a perpetual smile and a bright disposition, as if she carried a bit of her native Hawaiian Islands within her wherever she went. Though she'd been volunteering at FOF for some years now, I didn't know her well. There were so many tasks to choose from at the shelter, and where I was strictly hands-on with the cats, Alani had taken a job in the office, filing, scanning, and stuffing envelopes. I only saw her during lunch or at meetings and classes, so when she volunteered for the Starry Nights decorating team, I was thrilled.

"Robert is coming with the truck," Frannie said by way of a greeting. "He has the decorations."

"Except what we could fit in my car," Alani finished. "The more delicate items."

I rubbed my palms together wishing I'd worn gloves. At least today I'd opted for a heavier jacket, a red wool coat embroidered with holly leaves given to me by my mother. "And when can we expect our dear Robert?" I asked facetiously.

"He promised he'd be right along," said Alani, "but you look doubtful. You've done this before, I take it."

"A few times."

"He'll get here when he gets here," Frannie commented. "Meanwhile we can haul these things inside and unlock the loading bay doors."

"Ever the voice of reason," I laughed.

Alani had begun pulling boxes and flats of sparkly stuff from the front-end trunk of her little vehicle and handing them to Frannie and me. For a small car, it held quite a load, and by the time she was done, the three of us were heaped with cargo. Carefully we picked our way to the conference center entrance. I turned around, shoving one of the big glass double doors open with my backside. Alani caught it and held it for Frannie who had an odd-shaped bundle of human-sized standees—anthropo-morphized cats in romantic mediaeval costume. We crossed the lobby with its blue and teal carpeting and pushed through the second set of doors, then stopped dead.

The huge conference room looked more like an institution than a party hall. Six-foot plastic tables placed regular as soldiers and surrounded by industrial-style metal folding chairs filled the area. At the front was a long counter mounded with wires, cables, and controls for a giant television set that took up one whole wall like a shiny black movie screen. The lights were brash and fluorescent. Instead of holiday scent, the air smelled of freshener, the mildly toxic kind.

"I know I'm new to this gala thing," Alani gasped, "but I was picturing something a bit more inviting. What are we supposed to do with all these tables and chairs?"

I dropped my stuff on the nearest flat surface and

turned to look again. Nope, nothing had changed. We were still facing an area more fit for a real estate convention than a party.

A woman in a brown suit rushed in, out of breath. "Are you Friends of Felines?"

I nodded.

She held out a short-nailed hand and smiled, showing slightly horsey teeth. "Happy holidays. I'm Susan Ward, director. I'm so sorry I wasn't here to greet you."

"Hello, Susan," I said, shaking the hand and looking over the frazzled woman. She was middle-aged and well put together but still giving off the impression of chaos. Maybe it was the wild hazel eyes or the locks of gray-flecked orange hair escaping from her strict coif, but I had the feeling her job might be harder than most assumed.

"So Susan," I went on, "I wasn't the one who made arrangements, but this room doesn't seem right."

"In what way?" she asked, staring blankly around the sterile area.

"We rented it for a party, an upscale gala. This looks more suited to a conference."

Susan quickly checked her tablet. "Oh, dear! These should have been out of here long before now. You have round tables coming, and real chairs, wood with cushions." She flipped a few pages and held the board out to me, showing a nice squarish space with circles around the perimeter—the tables, I presumed—and a rectangle at one side signifying a stage.

I looked from the layout to the narrow room. "It doesn't seem big enough."

"That partition goes open..." She waved a hand at the fabric wall on our right. "...so you'll have twice the space. I'm so sorry! If you could just give me a few minutes, I'll get someone on it immediately."

She made a little gesture that could have been a curtsey or merely a uncomfortable squirm. "There's a coffee shop across the way if you'd like to wait there." She rummaged in a pink portfolio she carried at her side and pulled out a pad of paper. Whipping off three squares and initialing with a quick squiggle, she handed them to me. "Breakfast is on us."

I took the coupons with a thank you.

"What should we do with our things?" Frannie asked, juggling her standees into a more comfortable position.

"Just leave them—they'll be fine. Here's my card if you need anything else. Anything at all," she added, giving me a pleading look.

"Alright," I replied. "Thanks."

"No, thank *you* for being so accommodating. The Bremerton prides itself on customer service. I don't know why your rooms weren't ready first thing this morning," she said, a dark look descending over her carefully made-up face, "but I promise I'll find out."

After Alani deposited her boxes on a table and Frannie propped the cat standees nearby, we made our way back outside and across the drive to the coffee shop. As I glanced back, Susan stood in the doorway. She was on the phone, gesticulating feverishly with her free hand. All graciousness had fled, and she looked mad as a wet cat.

Frannie caught my eye and followed it to the unhappy woman. "I wonder what happened. Arrangements for the fête were made months ago."

"Human error most likely. As long as they can fix it, I don't care."

"Stuff happens," said Alani. "Anyway I could do with a coffee."

We entered the homey café, stomping the thin film of ice from our boots on the mat. The place was small and packed with breakfasters, but there was a free table at the back and we took it eagerly.

The scent of eggs and hot coffee combined with the relaxing warmth was immediately inviting, though I couldn't say the same of the decor. Someone had bought up a Walmart's-worth of colored Christmas lights and hung them everywhere: from the ceiling; above the tables; outlining the booths. The artwork, whatever it may have been originally, was now wrapped with cheap holiday paper and tied with big bows to resemble Christmas presents. The piece at our table had red reindeer patterned against wavy green holly, but rather than giving me a happy holiday glow, it only served to remind me I had more Christmas shopping to do.

When the server came, we all ordered coffee and waffles, figuring this was a good opportunity to fortify ourselves with maple syrup energy for the hours of setup to come. Somehow we had to turn that artless hall into a wonderland befitting the name of Starry Nights. If I didn't know the magical skills of a persistent crew of volunteers, I would have been at my wits' end.

The front door tinkled, and in came another member of our group, Delaney Davis. Delaney, forty-five with the energy of a fifteen-year-old, was a real catch for the decorating team because not only was she an artist in her own right, she did this sort of thing all the time. Party planning was more of a hobby with her than an occupation since she made a good living with her feline-themed collages, but she told me once she had three loves: her art, her cats, and putting on a great party.

I hadn't realized how stressed I'd been until that

moment, but with one look at the boxy figure with her short blue hair and her pack full of magical tricks, I found myself giving a huge sigh of relief. I scooched over and made room for her in our booth. Delaney sat, greetings were made, and another cup of coffee was ordered.

"The woman in the hall sent me over here," she said, embracing the restaurantware mug like a long-lost friend. "Something about the room still being prepared?"

"When we got here, it was set up for a business conference." Alani described our shock at finding the cramped and barren space. "Someone forgot to do their homework."

"Well, it's looking good now," Delaney announced. "They're just bringing in the tables. They asked what coverings we'd like, and I chose the dark blue. Hope that's okay. I figured anything but the usual red and green."

"You're the artist," I said around a mouthful of thick waffle lavished with sticky syrup. "But I was under the impression that had already been arranged."

She threw up a hand, a cluster of diamonds and gold flashing from her ring finger. "Oh, you know how it is. Everything last minute."

The door jangled once more, and Susan Ward stuck her head in. She gazed around the room until she caught our eye, then waved and called out, "Ready when you are. Thanks again for being so flexible, and welcome to the Bremerton Inn."

* * *

How it comes about that a bare, blank room can be transformed in mere hours to a world of wonder by a group of volunteers wielding little more than cheap decorations and team spirit never ceases to amaze me.

Once Robert arrived with the truck full of draperies, sparkly trim, dangling stars, and an assortment of lights, it hadn't taken long for the chaos to begin to morph into a holiday landscape. Robert had helped Alani hang the stars and garlands—in spite of her full figure, the young volunteer had no fear of heights, swarming the towering equipment like a cat up a tree. Delaney oversaw the placement, devising ingenious and unique ways to hang, affix, and layer the ornamentation without breaking any of the hotel rules. By early afternoon, there was nothing left of the dry conference arena we'd come upon that morning.

"What say we break for lunch?" Frannie suggested, untying her apron strings—leave it to Frannie to supply her own stylish holiday apron patterned with bows, stars, and cats.

She tossed the garment on a chair, then turned and surveyed the room. I stood beside her, taking in the amazing transformation. From out of confusion, a magical winterland was emerging. It wasn't quite there yet—tablecloths and centerpiece arrangements had yet to be distributed, and the room was still cluttered with tools and equipment—but the theme was set, a picture postcard of Christmas past.

"Will it be ready in time?" I asked doubtfully.

"Of course."

"How can you be so sure?"

"How can you not? You've done this before. You know it always comes together." Frannie looked at me. "What's going on, Lynley? It isn't like you to be so gloomy."

I turned away, picked up a box of jar candles and then put them down again. "Oh, I don't know. It's the season, I suppose. People stealing cats, people disappearing—it just doesn't feel like Christmas."

"I know you're worried about Isis, but who else has disappeared?"

"Cat Black never came back for her van last night. It was still parked in front of my house this morning when I left. I'm worried about her."

Frannie's brow furrowed. "Is there anyone you can call? A partner or roommate?"

"I called Special Agent Connie. She said she'd check."

"Then I'm sure she will." Frannie took my arm. "Now how about that break? The coffee shop for a bowl of soup or a sandwich?"

"I'm still full from waffles, but another cup of coffee might be nice."

Even though it was only a short walk across the roadway, we donned coats and hats and were thankful we had when we emerged from the conference center to find it had begun to snow again. This time it looked like it was serious about it—flakes falling in an ever-increasing number, the midday darkened to dusk by a slate-gray sky. The wind was beginning to pick up as well, blasting the chill in our faces. We hurried into the coffee shop, shivering and glad of the food-scented warmth.

We found a booth with a window view of the parking lot and were settling when the door crashed open and a stocky woman blustered through. Special Agent Connie Lee stomped the snow off her regulation boots, then scanned the room, her gaze quickly lighting on me.

"Lynley!" she called out as she bee-lined over. "Just dropping off our donation for the raffle tonight. They told me you were here."

"Connie, what's up? Have you heard from Cat?"

Connie slipped in beside me, not bothering to shed her blue uniform coat in spite of the brushing of snow on each shoulder. The equipment on her duty belt clattered as she made herself comfortable. She waved to the server and mouthed the word *coffee*. The server nodded and went for the pot.

"No word on Cat," Connie growled. "No word on Isis. Nothing." She swore, slapping a gloved hand on the Formica table just as the coffee came. The server gave her a surprised look. "Sorry, ma'am," Connie said as she took the steaming mug and set it down. "Thanks."

"So what now?"

Connie pulled off her gloves and strapped them to her jacket. Taking a slurp of coffee, she shook her head. "I don't know, Lynley. Cat hasn't been gone long enough for it to be a missing persons case. And she is an artist, which means she can be unpredictable. But this doesn't feel right. She wouldn't just leave her car and go off the grid with Isis lost like that."

For a moment, the three of us were silent. I was contemplating the possibilities, aghast at how unprepared I was to deal with any of the scenarios that came to mind. Then I heard the familiar buzz of a cell phone. Looking around at Frannie and Connie, I realized it was mine.

"Sorry," I said, digging the offending instrument out of my purse. I wasn't militant about no phones in a restaurant, but I knew others were. Still, this was a hotel café, not the Ritz, and I wasn't the only one chatting or texting or surfing away their lunch hour. Besides, with all that was going on, I was curious as to who would be calling.

Checking the display, I saw it was an unfamiliar number. Probably a solicitor asking for money or a spam scam telling me there was a problem with a credit card I didn't own. I nearly put it away unanswered, but something told me it might be important.

"Hello?" I said tentatively.

At first there was no sound on the line. I waited for the inevitable click of the robot call to switch on, but instead I heard a soft voice, very faint, a whisper:

"Lynley Cannon? Lynley? Is that you?"

Chapter 9

Snow globes can be deadly to animals because the liquid inside contains antifreeze which is extremely toxic if swallowed or even licked. If a snow globe gets broken, clean up the contents completely and keep pets away from the area.

"Yes, it's Lynley. Who's this?"

There was another pause, long enough to again make me consider hanging up. But I didn't.

Finally, "It's Cat. Cat Black. Are you alone?"

A spike of adrenaline coursed through me. "No, I'm in a coffee shop with a friend. Connie's here too. Would you like..."

"Don't tell her it's me!" Cat hissed. "Don't tell anyone. Sorry, Lynley, but this is important."

I tried to keep my face expressionless as I politely excused myself from the table. To Connie, who had looked up at the mention of her name, I mouthed, "Work"—probably not the smartest fib since it went nowhere to explain my reference to her. That and the fact both Frannie and the special agent knew I'd been retired for years rendered my excuse less than plausible, but it was all I could come up with on demand.

"Okay, hold on," I told the mysterious Cat.

I walked down the aisle to the café entrance. There was a pink Naugahyde bench near the door, empty at the moment, so I sat. It wasn't all that private, but I was darned if Cat's cryptic mandate for secrecy would get me outside in the snow.

"What's going on, Cat? We've been worried. You left your van..."

"I don't have much time," she interrupted. "I need you to do something for me."

"Are you alright?" I waved innocently to Frannie and Connie who were watching me like cats on a bird.

"Never mind that now. I'm with Isis. Well, not literally but I know where she is. She's here. If I can just..."

"Cat, slow down. You're not making sense."

Instead of an explanation, she blurted, "I thought I could do this on my own, but, well, turns out I can't." I heard a short sob, then she was all business again. "Now listen carefully. I need you to come to where we are. I need you to bring money. You won't be in danger—you can just drop it off and go back home again."

"So someone really did cat-nap Isis? Is it about Wicca?"

"Maybe—maybe not. They're holding her for ransom. But now they've got me too."

"Who? Who's got you?" On a shelf nearby was a collection of snow globes. Absentmindedly I picked one up and examined the miniature scene of a village church.

"I... I don't know. A man, or men. I've only seen one guy but he alluded to a partner. He's disguised with a funny mask, one of those rubber things with horns and a Santa hat. They have Isis locked away, and he said if he can't persuade me to pay out, he'll turn us over to someone who can, someone willing to pay extra for his trouble."

I shook the globe, watching the swirl of fake snow engulf the tiny steeple. "This horned guy, where is he

75

now?"

"Someone left in a car, then nothing for a long time. Now the car's come back but no one's looked in on me." She faltered. "I've made a mess of things. Oh, Lynley, you've got to bring the money! It's my only hope to make things right."

"Slow down, Cat. I'll do what I can, but I'm confused. Make things right? What things?"

"I don't have time for this," Cat cried.

"If you want my help," I said bluntly, "then make time."

She sighed. "Alright, if you insist."

"I do. Begin with when you left my house. You were going to the store?"

"I was. I'd just walked in when I got a call from a man telling me he had Isis, and if I ever wanted to see her alive, to be on the corner of Thirty-eighth and Stark with twenty-thousand cash. I didn't believe him at first, but he was very convincing." She paused for a breath. "I told him no cash until I saw Isis and made sure she was okay, and he agreed. He picked me up, put a bag over my head, and drove me here."

"Where's here?"

"I'm not sure. Bag? Head? Remember? But it's out of town, an abandoned gas station at the end of a road, really old, looks like it went out of business years ago." She faltered. "Me coming empty-handed was not what he'd had in mind. That's when things sort of fell apart."

"You didn't take the money?"

"I had other plans for getting Isis back."

"Plans? What sort of plans?"

"Never mind that now. Suffice it to say they didn't work. When the masked guy found out there was no money, he got really mad and shoved me into the back, the mechanics shop, except there's nothing left but the bay where they used to fix the cars."

"Is that where you are now?"

"No, I picked the lock with a saw blade I found on the floor and managed to get into the office. There's a working landline telephone here, a couch, file cabinet. There are blankets and empty takeout boxes—looks like someone's been living here."

"Can you get out?"

"The door's locked with a deadbolt. Besides, I'm not leaving without Isis."

"But Cat, I don't get it. Why call me?"

"He took my cell with all my contacts in it," she huffed in frustration, "but I still have your card. Sorry, Lynley, but it has to be you."

"Special Agent Connie's right here. Don't you think she'd be better suited..."

"No! No cops. Please Lynley. North Willow Bluff Road is what's painted on the front window. I don't know where that is but you can look it up. There's a mailbox out front, one of those rural ones on a post. Put the money in that."

"How much?" I found myself saying against all my better judgment, "and where do I get it?"

"I have money, not what they asked for, but maybe it'll be enough. It's in my van, my life's savings, in a hideaway under the seat. Just bring it all."

"You keep your money in your van?"

"I don't trust banks," she answered brusquely.

A couple passed by me as they left the café, but it wasn't the icy gust sweeping in through the open door on their departure that made me shiver. I replaced the snow globe on the shelf and slipped out behind them.

"So let me get this straight, Cat. You want me to collect money from your van and drive out to the boonies to drop it in a mailbox. Then what?"

"Then you turn around and go home again. And don't tell a soul until you hear from me."

"Why can't I just call the police and have them swarm the place?"

"No! No, you can't! Isis... Isis..."

Suddenly there was only silence.

"Cat? You still there?"

I heard a clatter—the handset being dropped on a hard surface? Through the line I made out what sounded like a scuffle, then a sharp scream and something heavy falling to the floor, like a body.

"Cat! Cat, are you alright?"

Nothing, then a click. I looked at the phone display but I didn't need to see the hang-up symbol to know the call had disengaged.

I stood, letting the snow dot my shoulders, wondering what to do now. I'd forgotten the cold, forgotten my friends inside, forgotten everything except the enigma that was Cat Black. If she'd wanted to pay the ransom, why hadn't she taken the money with her in the first place? Had she really thought she could defeat the cat-nappers and rescue Isis all by herself? Would the partial payment appease the kidnapper, or would he still hand them off for the promised extra cash?

More immediate questions loomed however, the big one being, was I going to do as she asked? I looked at the snow flurries which were coming down harder now. I didn't like driving in icy conditions at the best of times, and though it was still early, the sky was beginning to darken—night would be upon us soon. The thought of a trip alone into the snowy wilderness was so far beyond my comfort zone I felt a zing of anxiety just contemplating it. As an anxiety sufferer, I have to watch the signs and be careful not to trigger a panic episode which can incapacitate me for weeks on end. No, I wouldn't do it. I *couldn't* do it. Cat Black was asking too much.

Then I remembered Isis, a sweet innocent cat caught up in the wicked plans of humans. With a sigh, I knew I would be taking the trip after all.

I returned to my table and collected my things, trying to evade the questioning glances.

"Something's come up," I said as I shrugged into my coat. "I've got to go."

Frannie and Connie Lee stared at me in disbelief.

"But what about the set-up?" Frannie burst out.

Rats, the fête. I couldn't believe it had slipped my mind. "I'm sorry to bail, but things seem to be going well in there. I'm sure Delaney will have everything ready by show time."

"Okay," Frannie said doubtfully, "I guess..."

"Is there a problem?" Connie probed. "You look upset."

"No, nothing," I replied way too fast. "Well, yes, but it's personal."

I said my goodbyes, put a five down for my coffee and tip, and started for my car. Frannie followed and once we were outside, she grabbed me by the arm.

"Lynley, what's the matter? You're white as the snow."

"It's..." How could I tell my best friend and confidant that this time my secret couldn't be shared? "Can we talk about it later?"

Frannie frowned, then forced a smile. "Of course we can. I'll see you tonight. You can tell me then."

"Tonight?" I answered stupidly.

"At the fête," She declared.

I shook my head, trying to rattle some sense back into my brain. "Yes, the fête. Yes, right. I'll be there."

She looked at me, her blue-gray eyes filled with concern. "Why wouldn't you?"

I gave her an impulsive kiss on the cheek and turned for my car.

Chapter 10

What types of animals may be a witch's familiar? Familiar spirits are commonly small animals, such as cats, rats, dogs, ferrets, birds, frogs, toads, and rabbits, but there are also cases of wasps, butterflies, pigs, sheep, and horses filling the position.

This was going to be ugly. Even the drive from the Bremerton Inn toward home was challenging. The snow wasn't sticking on the main roads, but people were already going crazy in anticipation. That, and the layer of last night's ice caused a very real danger. Many workplaces had let employees off early to avoid being stranded, and the additional traffic made matters worse. It was a slow, hazardous crawl, but when I wasn't tapping my brakes or fearing for my life, it gave me time to think.

Cat was in trouble. Though our conversation had been cryptic and lacking in a few important details, I had no doubt she was in over her head. Someone was holding her for ransom, or more accurately, holding Isis. What's more, they were ready to sell them on to a higher bidder if Cat didn't come through with the cash. The priestess and her familiar. On the night of the Winter Solstice. It could be anyone, but I kept coming back to the Twenty-two Eighteens.

Suddenly I made a decision. I changed my course and headed for St Joseph's Memory Care Center. I wanted to talk to Melody again. It was doubtful she could tell me what I needed to know—heck, I didn't even know what I needed to know—but I had a feeling if anyone could help right now, she might be the one.

"I'm here to see Melody," I told the older man at the admittance desk as I signed in on the clipboard. He gave me a funny look. "It's Lynley Cannon."

A spark of recognition crossed his ruddy face. "Oh, yeah. You look different."

"No cat," I shrugged.

"That must be it. She's in her room. You know the drill."

Melody invited me in after a series of knocks. She was seated by the window in her wheelchair, which since my last visit had been done up with layers of garlands and blinky holiday lights.

"I was dozing," she said sleepily.

"I'm sorry to wake you, but I have something I'd like to talk to you about. Is now a good time?"

"I've got nothing but time." She peered at me as I sat down on the ottoman in front of her. "I'm sorry. Who are you?"

"It's Lynley. I was here yesterday with Tinkerbelle. Tinkerbelle the cat?" I repeated to the blankness of her stare.

I reached into my purse and pulled out my phone, flipped through the photos until I came to a shot of the black therapy cat, and held it out for her to see. A big grin blossomed on her face. She looked up at me and then around, as if expecting to see the real cat.

"I didn't bring her this time. It's just me."

"Oh," she said rather sadly.

I figured I should come straight to the point and took the framed picture of her in the Wiccan robe from the bookshelf.

"We were looking at this yesterday. Do you remember?"

"I remember the picture, honey. Me when I was young. A long time ago."

"You were a witch."

"Yes," she said gleefully. "Still am."

She gestured to the corner of the room where, nestled in the shadows, was a small altar. A pink, beaded pentagram hovered above a collection of objects—a rock, a shell, a feather, and an unlit votive candle. "Does that shock you?"

"No, in fact I find it very interesting. I have another friend who is a witch, a high priestess of her coven. She has a cat..."

"A familiar, yes. Cats make very good familiars. They don't have to be black, you know. That's nonsense."

"This one is Siamese."

"Ah, appropriate," she exclaimed. The coloring, you see, represents both the dark and the light."

"Huh," I mused. "I'd never thought of that. Anyway," I pushed on, not wanting to get the old woman sidetracked on the meaning of coat coloration, "my friend and her cat, her familiar, are supposed to participate in the Winter Solstice celebration. Do you know much about that?"

"Oh, yes. It's an important time for us. Without the priestess to guide the coven, the ritual will fail to bring the light. The year following will go badly."

"How badly?"

"Very badly." She shivered. "When Evil awakens, only Good can drive it back from mortal shores."

I paused, musing on how to word this next question.

So far she was doing brilliantly, but one never knew when the confusion of dementia might return.

"What would happen if the high priestess and her familiar were, say, prevented from performing the ritual?"

"Prevented?"

"Say, someone held them hostage so they couldn't take part."

"The priestess is essential for the Return of the Light." She paused. "Did you say they were hostage?"

"Let's just say, what if?"

Her rheumy eyes went wide, as if she were seeing something hateful. Her mouth opened but no sound came out.

"Melody, what is it? You're scaring me."

Her head snapped around. I could see terror etched in every muscle of her face.

"It is said," she intoned, "that if the priestess is held from the circle against her will, if priestess and familiar together are bereft of consciousness, then... then..."

"Bereft of consciousness—as in drugged? Knocked out?"

She just stared at me.

"Dead?"

She nodded.

"So if someone wanted to sabotage the Winter Solstice ritual, they might do it by harming the priestess and her familiar?"

"'When Evil holds the longest night,'" she chanted, "'then Good will forfeit sacred light.'"

"What does that mean?"

"The spirits of darkness will swarm forth!" she pronounced in a voice so low and guttural I hardly believed it was her own.

84

"Is that a real thing, or part of the ritual myth?"

"Myth..."

"It's a myth?"

"Myth," she repeated slowly, her tongue curling around the word as if it were foreign to her.

"Yes, the spirits of darkness? We were talking about the Winter Solstice ritual. The high priestess and her familiar? Remember?"

"Myth," she said for a third time.

The room was darkening as the day faded to night, but I could still see her face in the glow of the Christmas lights. It was utterly vacant.

* * *

Melody's remarks plagued me on my way home. All I'd really wanted to know was if there could be a reason for the anti-pagans to capture Cat and Isis. Apparently there was, and it could involve physical abuse... or death. *They wouldn't go that far, would they?* But then Melody's tales of Wicca had drifted between reality and fantasy. Maybe she was wrong about that part; maybe the only reason the anti-pagans wanted the pair was for harassment or cash. Either way, there was little I could do but deliver the money to the kidnapper and pray for the best.

Once home, I pulled in behind Cat's van. Staring at the vehicle that was beginning to resemble a white-iced loaf cake, I realized I'd completely forgotten to ask Cat how I was to get inside. Was it too much to hope that she had left it unlocked?

Stepping gingerly out of my car, I half-shuffled, half-slid up to the passenger side and tried the handle. Yup, way too much to hope. The little black knob on the other side was pushed down as well. A tiny voice in my head said, *Yay! Now I have an excuse not to go.* But that wouldn't work. Cat and Isis were in danger, and if I didn't take the money, who knew what the cat-napper-turned-kidnapper might do with them.

I heard the slam of a door and looked over to see Fredric, sans elf costume, come bouncing down the front steps of his duplex. He waved and I waved back. He began to turn away, off to some curious and colorful destination I guessed from knowing the young man, but then he glanced back. Changing directions, he ventured over.

"What's up, Lynley? You look concerned."

"I need to get into this van but it's locked. I don't suppose you know how to break into cars," I said wistfully.

"Why? What's in there?"

"Money, if you must know. A friend—the owner of the car—needs it."

He turned his attention to the van. "Doesn't this belong to the lady who makes the cat towers? The Wiccan?"

"That's the one."

"It's been here a while. I'm surprised Mr. Foley hasn't got the cops out to give it a ticket."

"I am too, as a matter of fact. The police are probably too busy to come by, what with the bad weather."

Fredric walked to the back of the van and considered it from that end. "So why is it still here?"

"She's... delayed... somewhere. That's why she needs me to get the *thing* for her."

"The money thing?"

"Yeah." I knew I was sounding overly mysterious, but I was really trying to do as Cat asked. Lying wasn't something that came naturally to me, and the worldly Fredric would catch me out in a minute. "I was told not to talk about it. Thanks anyway."

Fredric eyed me up and down. "Be right back."

He boot-skied over to his car, rummaged through the trunk, and returned with a slim jim.

He juggled it in his hand. "You really want me to do this?"

I gritted my teeth, understanding that once I got the money, there would be no turning back. "Go ahead, do it."

Fredric slipped the instrument down between the window glass and the door panel, and in a matter of seconds, had the big door unlocked. He pulled it open with a metallic creak, scattering snow on the parking strip. "There you go. Need me to commit any other illegal acts while I'm here?"

"No thank you," I replied with a smile, "and I won't enquire how you learned to do that."

"I'm a man of many talents, M'lady," he replied in his newfound elfin accent.

Reaching into the cab of the older van, I felt around under the seat and came up empty. Pulling myself inside, the scent of incense hitting me with a hippie flashback, I investigated beneath the driver's seat. My hand met with cold, slick resistance—the money box!

"Ow!" I exclaimed as I bent a fingernail trying to pry it from its hiding place. "It's stuck."

"Here, let me." Fredric didn't wait for an answer but reached through, unlocked the rear door, and jumped into the back. Winding around lengths of wood, climber parts, a small tree trunk, and other building miscellanea, he bent down and peered under the seat. Then with both hands, he reached in and pulled. The thing slipped out easily, revealing itself to be an antique metal strongbox.

He held it up to his ear and rattled it, receiving a shuffling sound, the kind made by papers—or bills. He jumped from the vehicle and handed it to me. I tried the latch but it didn't open. *Great!* I thought to myself. *Another lock to pick.*

"How are you with strongboxes?" I asked the young man.

Fredric took it back, studied the latch, then in a decisive move, leaned over and banged the right front corner on the curb. The lock popped open as if by magic.

He gave me a wry smile. "Don't ask about that one either, okay?"

"Never."

He flipped the lid and we both gave a gasp. There, in crisp new-bound stacks, were at least a dozen packets of hundred dollar bills.

Chapter 11

How far would you go to protect your cat from harm? I think most cat people will say they would do whatever it takes. This protective reaction is not beyond reason: when we adopt an animal into our family, we assume the responsibility for that life.

What could be more nerve-wracking than driving alone in the snow, in the dark, up a strange back road, with twelve-thousand dollars in my car? Nothing I could think of right off the bat. Yet there I was, doing just that.

Night had fallen, and it was black as a Bombay cat once away from the city lights. I'd looked up the street name Cat had given me, and found it was out past Canby: south on the freeway, east on the highway, off a major street, then down a smaller road and another. The snow had escalated, blowing sideways and hitting my windshield wipers like a curtain of stars. It reminded me of the psychedelic Star Gate scene from 2001 Space Odyssey, the part we all looked forward to when we were young and stoned. Luckily my wipers were new and efficient, whisking away the wowie-zowie factor at half-second intervals.

Google had guided me to North Willow Bluff Road, but since I didn't know my destination address, I was now on my own. Uneasy at the best of times about going somewhere new, I was finding this trip agonizing. With the snowfall shrouding my view, I was worried I'd drive right by it. Cat said the abandoned gas station was on a dead end. What did that mean? Would I be stuck, literally, in the midst of snowy nowhere?

The farther I drove, the deeper the white stuff got. My speed had gradually declined, but since mine was the only car on the road, it didn't make much difference. This really was the countryside, with houses few and far between. Then I saw it, a sweep of white cutting off from the road and diverting underneath a covered area—the gas station's pull-through lane.

Thankfully the snow seemed to be letting up a little. I slid to a stop and looked closer. The gas pumps were gone, but the canopy remained, attached to the old building. All I could make out was a green door and the blaze of my headlights reflected back at me from a big front window. No lights inside. For a moment I wondered if this were the place, but then how many abandoned gas stations could there be on Willow Bluff?

I maneuvered the car into the pull-through and stopped, glad of the dry, black pavement under my tires. For a while I sat there, unsure what to do next. I kept an eye on the window, hoping for some sign of Cat. That had to be the office, didn't it? Was she there, gazing out at me from the darkness? But our phone call had ended abruptly with sounds of a struggle. I could only guess what had befallen the young Wiccan, and it was nothing good. Unless I wanted to play some kind of hero, I'd be better off following instructions and staying out of it.

So back to plan A. Most county boxes were alongside the road where the postal worker could get to them with their right-hand-drive car, but under the accumulation of snow, it could have been any of several white mounds I saw clustered there. Backing up, I cast my headlights in that direction and picked out a likely lump at the edge of the drive. Yes, I recognized the four-by-four base protruding beneath the cottony hood. I sighed with relief, then looked again and my heart fell. There were not one but three identical bases interspersed along the row of snow-bound humps. I felt a jab of panic. How could I know which mailbox belonged to the gas station? If I chose the wrong one, the money would be lost. The kidnapper would think Cat hadn't complied with his requests. She and Isis could be in more danger than ever.

An ancient derelict up on blocks underneath an awning was the only car in sight, but a set of tracks ran like twin black snakes from the road down past the building. The returning car? It looked like it had paused near the first box. I peered closer to note footprints mulling around the base. That had to be the one.

I turned off the ignition and let my surroundings settle into complete country dark. As my eyes adjusted, I caught the faintest glow coming from within the building, not the main office but somewhere behind. Had they noticed me? Heard me drive up? But of course they had. What criminal in his right mind wouldn't be alert to every little change in his environment?

I'd already decided my best move was to drop the ransom and run, but hovering in the back of my mind like a haloed conscience-angel was the thought that, while there, I should at least try to connect with Cat and Isis. If the ransom didn't do the trick, they would need help; if it did, they could probably use a ride home.

I took a deep breath, trying to wrestle my anxious thoughts into line. Mailbox, or go inside? I looked again at the patch of light emanating from within the bowels of the building. I thought I saw a flicker, as if someone were moving around. Cat? But no. If it were Cat, she would give me a sign. More likely the kidnapper waiting for me to deliver his money.

Instantly I came upon a new plan. I would put the money in the mailbox as ordered, pretend to pull away, then park and wait off to the side, keeping an eye out for the retrieval. Maybe once he got what he wanted, he would release Cat and Isis. Maybe Cat would come herself to get the money, and I could apprise her of my presence. Maybe aliens or zombies or vampires would rush in to probe or brain or bleed the villains who were putting a woman and a kitty through such a terrible ordeal!

I stashed my purse under the seat, grabbed the Tyvek bag in which I'd sealed Cat's money for safe keeping, and got out. For a moment, I stared into the night, waiting for my eyes to adapt. Though all I could see was black and white, shadows and silver, the snow reflected the ambient light with enough brilliance to make the way maneuverable.

I tested the slippery factor and was disheartened to find a slick layer of ice underneath the snow. As long as I utilized a precise stomping motion, I should be okay though. Yes, it probably looked funny to anyone watching—an old lady in a red coat marching through the virgin drifts—but it worked, and that was all that mattered.

The mailbox hunkered by the roadside like Casper the Friendly Ghost—only a short few feet away. I headed straight for it and was doing well when I felt my foot come down on a ridge, the edge of the asphalt pavement. Squirming the toe of my boot onto the new surface, I surmised it to be gravel. That shouldn't be a problem—I was about halfway to my goal. Just a few drifts and I'd be there.

I realized the minute I felt the ground disappear from under me that I had made a grave mistake. It had been a long time since I'd lived in the country, but wasn't there always a ditch between the road and the yard? That *duh* moment hit me as I felt myself lurch, topple, fall. I watched as the snow came up fast toward my face, thinking in that split second how soft it looked, yet pondering what hard, sharp, or otherwise injurious objects might be hidden underneath.

I slammed down, my glasses flying from my face and a sharp pain blooming from the side of my head. The momentum of my dive flipped me over, and I rolled. And rolled. My knee bashed against a boulder and my foot wedged into a crevice. As my body propelled downward, my ankle wrenched sideways, and all the other pains fled under the assault of that one complete agony.

I came to rest at the bottom of the ditch, staring up at glitter-spangled night. The snow had ceased altogether, but the heartbeat flashes of white-hot misery rivaled the pinpoint stars beginning to appear in the sky. I must have passed out for a moment, because when I next opened my eyes, I was staring up at a face.

I blinked, not understanding what I was seeing—this pale, wrinkled, loathsome, out-of-focus visage swimming in my misery-filled delusion. I tried to sit up and screamed, whether from pain or fear I couldn't guess.

The face disappeared, leaving only blackness.

I screamed again.

* * *

When next I came aware, I was still lying down but no

longer in the snowy ditch. I vaguely remembered being dragged roughly from my frozen resting place and deposited here, wherever here was. My head pounded but the throbbing in my ankle was worse. Just to be fair, there was something amiss with my knee as well. It felt swollen and puffy as an overripe grapefruit. Unfortunately it was the opposite leg from the twisted ankle so walking, let alone running away, seemed pretty much out of the question.

The room was dark save for a fuzzy honey light coming from somewhere behind me. I tried to turn, but my head swam with the movement. I felt for my glasses, realized they were missing, and instantly understood why I was seeing fuzz. I'm not blind without them, but what should have been crisp, clear images were reduced to patterns, colors, and shapes. Luckily I was pretty good at interpreting those shapes.

Unluckily, I had other problems.

"Just stay still," came a male voice from beyond my field of vision.

Adrenaline shot through me, and I struggled to rise. The chemical surge got me half-way there before the pain took over, but at least I could make out the speaker, the same grotesque face that had confronted me in the ditch. I concluded now that it was a mask, not a monster.

"Who are you? Where's Cat?"

"I'm here, Lynley," Cat said softly from the shadows.

I strained my eyes through the darkness and finally picked out a silhouette against the window.

"I told you to leave the money and go," Cat said flatly as she took a step toward me, a light-colored feline with dark points draped across her shoulders like a shawl. "You were never meant to get hurt." I couldn't see her face but the statement was cold, calculating, and utterly without fear.

"Cat? What the...?" I faltered, unable to put my chaotic thoughts into words. This made no sense. Why was she upset with me? In a sudden flash I wondered if for reasons unknown, Cat, herself, had masterminded this whole convoluted plan.

I looked back at the masked man.

That was when I saw the gun.

* * *

What I had mistaken for fearlessness in Cat's tone was in fact a state of terror so acute it had induced insensibility. How long had she been in the eye of that lethal weapon? How long had she endured the moment-to-moment threat of becoming dead?

I, on the other hand, seemed to have had all the fear knocked out of me. All I could think of was how silly the skinny man looked in his devil mask and Santa hat, and how mad I was about losing my glasses.

"Where's the money?" the monster growled. "Is this a trick?"

"No trick," said Cat. "She was supposed to bring it with her."

"I did bring it, Devil-boy," I said. "I was taking it to the mailbox as instructed, but I slipped. I'm old. Old people slip sometimes."

I heard a growl from behind the plastic mouth. "It's Krampus, not the devil, you silly cow."

"Cow?" I huffed. "Well, I'd rather be a cow than a Cramp-whatever."

"*Krampus*. Don't you know who Krampus is?"

I shook my head, careful not to start up the throbbing

again. His voice was boyish, and somehow familiar. Elvis from the anti-witch boycott? Or maybe the more militant Isaac?

"Krampus is a demon, Santa's alter ego. He's the one who punishes bad kids when they misbehave. And I mean really punishes them. Like I'm going to punish both of you for not bringing me my money."

"Hold on." I raised a palm, noticing as I did the sting of a scrape, another injury from my swan dive. "I had it. I must have dropped it in the ditch."

"I didn't see anything," the man shot back. He looked between Cat and me. "You're trying to cheat me."

"No," Cat countered.

"You should have followed directions," he spat. "You've been messing with me all along."

"No," she persisted, but I could tell her facade of strength was beginning to crack. As she stepped into the glow of ambient light, I saw blood on her face. "It's true I lied about having it with me when you picked me up, but I'm not playing you now, I swear. I hoped I could talk you out of it, that if you knew my story, you'd understand. It's my life savings, everything I have."

"That's not what I hear. I heard you were rich, that you have an inheritance worth millions. Half a mil is just a drop in the bucket. Don't lie to me."

"An inheritance?" Cat choked. "Where did you get that idea?"

The kidnapper declined to answer.

"Let me guess. You found out my full name is Bremerton-Black and assumed because I'm related to rich people, I'm in line for their wealth. Well, your information's way off. My immediate family is still alive and in good health, and when they do go, I'll be lucky to inherit anything but debt. My dad's an artist and my mother's a writer. They live on social security in a commune."

I thought I saw the gun waver but then it snapped back front and center. "You're lying!"

"I'm not. Google Bremerton-Black. You'll find no mention of my branch of the family."

A sigh, rather like a pig-snort, came from the man. "Then give me what you got."

Again the three-way stare-fest. I didn't need my glasses to see Cat couldn't take much more. The kidnapper's mask gave nothing away, but I thought I detected a slouch to his stance that hadn't been there a minute ago.

"So?" he grumped.

"You're the one who went to get Lynley," Cat said. "You didn't see it out there?"

The man huffed, "It's dark. Besides I thought it'd be in her pocket or something," he said pensively, sounding younger than ever.

"It's in a white Tyvek envelope," I ventured. "It's got to be in the snow near where I fell, along with my glasses. Maybe you should go look. Now."

"Shut the quack up!" he yelled.

For a moment, nobody moved, then he lowered the gun and stuck it in the back of his jeans. "Okay, but I'm taking that cat with me."

He crossed the room in two long strides and wrenched a protesting Isis from Cat Black's neck. The girl screamed and reached out, but the kidnapper squeezed Isis in a malicious grip.

"Uh-uh-uh," he scolded, holding Isis by her scruff as he tucked her under his arm like a football. "Better not spook her—I might accidently *on purpose* let her go outside in the cold." He snickered. "You two behave yourselves. I won't be long."

A little bell over the door tinkled as he left. Cat ran to the window, watching helplessly. I sat up a bit straighter. My headache was beginning to diminish, and as long as I didn't move my legs, the knee and ankle were relatively benign. It was time to concentrate on getting some answers.

"Cat, are you okay? What happened? Did he hit you?"

She absentmindedly touched a head wound where the blood had dried into a red-black crust. "No, I slipped when we were wrestling for the phone. It probably looks worse than it is."

"Here, let me see."

"It's fine!" she snapped.

"If you say so," I replied, a bit taken aback by her vehemence, but then again, she must have been in shock.

I switched to another question on my mind. "You tried to talk him out of the ransom money? Did you really think that would work?"

Without taking her eyes off her cat, she said, "Yes, I really did. He sounded so polite on the phone. I thought if I could get him face to face, maybe he'd listen to me." She hesitated, then her voice lowered to a whisper. "And if that didn't work, Isis and I would take him on together..."

"Take him on? What do you mean?"

She turned to me, tears streaming down her cheeks. "I messed up, Lynley. I thought we'd have the power. It's a simple spell to bring the dark side into the light, embrace the truth, abandon the damaging path. Honesty and heart. I hoped that if he looked into his heart and was honest with himself, he wouldn't want to do this anymore. I was wrong."

"You put a spell on him?"

"We tried, but nothing happened. Usually there's some sort of change in the subject's demeanor." She paused. "He did seem a bit confused, but his purpose never wavered. The only thing I can imagine is that he must honestly need that money."

The honest villain? I wasn't so sure.

"You have a phone." I gestured to the vintage green dial-phone on the desk. "I still don't understand why you didn't call the police."

Krampus-boy was coming back now. He'd found the envelope and was struggling it open as he walked, a challenge with poor Isis locked under his arm. I saw no sign of my glasses.

"He threatened Isis," Cat blurted. "You, of all people, know I couldn't take that chance."

Chapter 12

How far would your cat go to protect you? Cats have been known to chase off other cats, dogs, and even people who threaten their cohabitor.

Krampus-boy was still wrestling with the envelope as he stumbled through the door. I've learned from experience there are only two ways to break the seal on those Tyvek folders: use a sharp instrument or take the time to seek out the obscure little *open here* tab. He seemed to be utilizing neither technique.

Dumping Isis on the desk, he went at it with both hands. I imagined his face under the mask as flushed and frustrated.

"Here, let me get that for you," I volunteered.

He stopped dead, seethed for a moment, then launched the package at me. I felt out the tab, pulled it, and voila! Turning the envelope upside-down, I let the bundles of money fall to the floor. Krampus-boy gave a little squeal and jumped for them.

I didn't know what our kidnapper had in store for us once he got what he wanted—he held all the cards in the form of the gun. Would he nicely let us drive back to town as he'd indicated? Or would he go ahead with his plan to sell Cat and Isis to the high bidder?

I couldn't take that chance. As he crouched down in front of me, I swung the better of my two injured legs, kicking him in the rubber forehead with my boot. He reeled backwards with a shriek. I let out a cry of my own as the impact stabbed through my hurt knee like a cat bite.

With a string of obscenities, some imaginative and some the classic, four-letter type, he reached behind his back for the gun. Another curse let me know it was no longer there.

I scanned the floor, dim in the dark, but all I could make out with my less-than-stellar eyesight was the expanse of plank floorboards. Krampus-boy had stopped blaspheming and was staring at Cat who was standing over him like a predator on prey. Isis was back around her neck. The gun was in her hand.

Then it wasn't.

Though blood trickled from under the kidnapper's mask onto his white tee shirt, the kick hadn't slowed him for long. With the grace of a panther, he leapt up and shoved Cat onto the desk. He grabbed the firearm, then with a little adrenaline-fueled shuffle, he turned and covered us both. Cat was struggling to regain her equilibrium while Isis vaulted onto a high filing cabinet, away from the fray. I sank back on the old couch. All I'd managed with my brave attack was to make our captor mad.

Krampus-boy seemed frozen in his defensive posture. He reminded me of one of those plastic toy soldiers the boys played with back in my day. Feet apart, arms spread, gun in hand, the gray, plastic figures had marched and fought at the hands of many a wannabe warrior. There were cowboy and Indian figures too, but those have become oh so politically incorrect. To note, I'd always sided with the Indians.

Suddenly through my nostalgia I registered that

though I was concerned and annoyed, I wasn't actually scared. A crazy man held a gun on me, and I wasn't even a little bit afraid. That made no sense. Either I was the crazy one or...

"You don't really want to be doing this, do you?" I asked pointedly.

The man gave a little "huh?" but his stance didn't falter.

"I mean, you obviously want the money... Need the money? But the rest of it, the inflicting of terror and pain, it's not really your thing." I paused. Something Cat had said about her spell of honesty and heart. "Your heart isn't in it. Am I right?"

Still no movement, but did I hear the ghost of a sigh?

"You don't have to do this, you know. You can still stop before any real harm is done. Let Cat and me go now—let us take Isis home. You'll have plenty of time to get away while we drive back to town. We don't know who you are. That Krampus mask has done its job, and we don't have a clue as to your identity."

The man stirred slightly. Was he thinking about it?

"I can tell you're not a bad person." How many times on television had I heard the good guy talk down the bad guy with those very words? It seemed a cliché. Hopefully Krampus-boy wouldn't find it so.

He continued to wave the gun between Cat and me, but it seemed as if it lingered in the harmless zone between the two of us for a longer time. He was thinking about it!

Then he turned his attention solely on Cat, the gun slack. "I..." he began, his voice cracking like a teenager. "I don't have any choice. I can't let you go."

"You have the money," I persisted. "It's cash and

probably not traceable. Come on. What's your option? Kill us?"

As soon as the words were out of my mouth, I regretted them. No reason to give the guy ideas.

There was a snuffling sound from behind the plastic mask. Was Krampus-boy crying?

"It's not enough," he whimpered. "Not nearly. I don't have a choice," he repeated. "This is all screwed up, but I can't stop now. I've got to go through with it. I don't want to but it's the only way.

"Yeah," he confirmed, as if he were trying to convince himself. "Yeah, that'll work." Standing straighter, he brought the gun up on Cat and said, "We're going for a ride."

"Wait! Where are you taking her?"

He paused. "I wasn't going to do it," he said almost apologetically. "I thought the guys were creeps. But I need that money badly. I'm sorry, but since you didn't come through with the whole amount, I've got to make it up somehow. They've offered big bucks if I can deliver you and the cat before midnight."

"Who?" I asked carefully, but I feared I already knew the answer. I also knew why. Melody had told me:

If the priestess is held from the circle against her will, if priestess and familiar together are bereft of consciousness...

* * *

Krampus-boy, now standing tall in the glow of his new plan, was met with a surprise. Though Cat had been subdued by his attack, she hadn't been idle. With a tiger cry, she raised her arm. She clutched something in her hand. I couldn't see what it was, but from the way she wielded it, I could tell it was heavy. A distinctive jingle marked it as the substantial desk phone. There's a use for those landlines yet!

She took a step forward and brought it down on Krampus-boy's face. I couldn't be sure, but it looked like it hit in about the same place my boot kick had landed earlier on. Ouch, that must have hurt!

Krampus-boy staggered. Cat cracked him again, and this time he went to his knees.

There was an explosion; I watched in horror as Cat stumbled and fell.

"Cat!" I cried. Had she been hit? I couldn't see. Curse my perilous eyesight!

"I'm okay," Cat panted. "He missed."

Krampus-boy was back on his feet, none too steady but making for the door. Then suddenly there was a flash and another tiger cry, this one the eerie war-wail of an enraged Siamese. The man went down face first. His forehead hit hard on the floor—a third blow to the kick site. He squirmed for a moment, then was still.

The ghostly streak split off from the inert body—Isis! The feline had tripped the criminal. How fitting, I thought to myself.

But no. Isis was still on her perch atop the file cabinet, motionless as a statue of Bast. Her face was in shadow but I could see her blue eyes glaring with a light of their own.

"Let's get out of here!" Cat shouted.

She rose and grabbed Isis, kicked the firearm under the file cabinet, then dashed to my side. Hauling me to my feet, she got an arm around my waist. We began for the door, but I stopped short when I caught sight of Krampus-boy. The mask had slipped, revealing a small neck tattoo. I reached down to pull back the disguise until I could see the face. Now I knew why the voice had seemed familiar.

Not Elvis or Isaac, not one of the protesters, but the holiday help from the Pet Pantry, Todd Tolliver.

Cat forced me away and we stumbled outside. In the distance I could hear sirens.

Chapter 13

Cats spend much of their time sleeping—up to eighteen hours a day! But there are several levels of sleep for the average cat, including the nap, the normal sleep, the deep sleep, and the times they fake sleep in order to ignore you. A cat who is upset by their situation, as when landing in a shelter, may sleep away the day, where one who has been through an ordeal, such as being lost, may seem almost catatonic when finally brought to safety.

Cat and I huddled in the front seat of my car. Isis had been relegated to the spare carrier I had stashed in my trunk in case I ran into any miscellaneous feline issues. She seemed happy for the quiet, fleece-lined isolation after her ordeal and had settled in for a nap, her brown heart face tucked neatly beneath a dark brown paw. I would have liked to have done the same, and Cat looked exhausted. Though her face was slack, her eyes were wide open, staring straight ahead like a zombie.

"You didn't have to call the police," Cat muttered, so low I could barely hear.

"You can't be serious," I gasped. "We could have been killed in there."

"We'd got him down. He wasn't going to come after us."

"We needed to preserve the crime scene so he can be charged for what he did. I, for one, don't like the idea of people thinking crime is the answer to their problems."

"Well, you really didn't have to tell them we'd wait, did you?" She sighed. "We could have been home by now."

I couldn't argue with her there. Once the police arrived and took control, there were the requisite interviews and paperwork, the medic check and victim blankets. The EMT had cleaned and bandaged Cat's head wound, then looked at my own bumps and bruises, wrapped my ankle, and asked if either of us wanted to go to the hospital. We declined. I don't know about Cat, but the last place I wanted to be was in some emergency waiting room.

Todd Tolliver had been treated for his facial abrasions, then cuffed and put in the back of a police cruiser where he also waited. I could see the silhouette of his bowed head through the back window.

"At least they found my glasses," I commented, thankful for the return of clear vision.

Cat lowered the window as an officer strode by. "Excuse me, but how much longer will you be holding us?"

The man stopped and gave Cat an ambiguous look. "I can't say, ma'am."

"Then who can? I have an important engagement, and so does my friend. We're the victims here, and it's long past time for us to go home."

"Yes, ma'am." He gave a nod. "Let me check for you."

Cat rolled up the window and settled back into the seat. The officer went away, hopefully in search of his superior.

"I still don't see why they won't give me my phone," she said sulkily. "What time is it?"

"Because it's evidence. It's got the call logs from the kidnapper. They have to go over all of that."

"But they let you have yours."

"Mine wasn't evidence. It's been in the car the whole time." I retrieved the instrument from the dash. "It's ten-thirty-two."

She squirmed in her seat. "After ten! Isis and I need to be preparing for the gift of the returning sun."

"And I'm missing the Starry Nights fête," I mourned, "after all the work I put into it."

"They can't keep us much longer, can they?"

"I'm sure they'll let us go soon," I told her, not sure at all, knowing from experience how long police procedure could take. At least this time no one was dead.

I looked outside the steamy windows. The pristine white surface of the driveway had been churned into a slushy mess of boot prints and vehicle tracks. Yellow crime scene tape cordoned off the entrance to the gas station even though there weren't any gawkers to hold at bay. Our officer was talking to a man in a suit. Then the two glanced back at us. The suit broke away and headed over. He was broad in the shoulders with a huge head and no neck. Former football player? All jowls and scowl. I worried for our fate.

Cat had no such qualms. Again she rolled down the window, letting in the cold of the night.

"Any news on our release?" she asked tersely.

"Ms. Black, Ms. Cannon," the man greeted with a formal nod. "Detective Omar Lowe. Sergeant Gilmore said you want to go home." He cracked a smile and his face did a complete turnabout. Maybe the scowl had been pretense, because this friendly visage seemed far more natural on him, reminiscent of a beardless Santa Claus.

"Very much so, Detective," I said across Cat. "Do you think you can arrange that for us?"

"You've both given your statements, correct?"

Cat nodded vigorously, and I said yes.

"And we have all your current information so we can reach you again?"

"Yes, everything."

"The medic released you?"

"We're fine," Cat broke in.

Lowe peered at my bandaged ankle. "You okay to drive, Ms. Cannon?"

"I'll drive," Cat volunteered before I could answer. "Please, can we go now?"

The big face sobered as if he were thinking hard, then softened again.

"I don't see why not. You ladies have a nice rest of your night."

I think we were both a little stunned by our brusque dismissal—at least I was. Cat hesitated only a millisecond before she jumped out of the car and came around to my side.

"Quick, hop into the passenger seat, before he changes his mind."

I didn't like the idea of a near stranger driving my car but had to admit if she were any kind of driver at all, she would do better than me with my fat ankle. I complied, handing her the keys and hobbling around the other side. She took the wheel, started the car, and was already pulling out as I was still closing my door.

I glanced back at the scene diminishing behind me, a pool of blazing light in a lake of darkness. I felt sad. I still couldn't believe it was Todd. The young man had seemed so positive, so pleasant. I hated that my intuition had got it so wrong.

I pointed Cat toward the highway and then was silent as she maneuvered the snowy roads. She seemed to be a safe driver, keeping a cautious pace, but I was nervous all the same. As soon as we hit the main road the snow and ice were gone, the traffic having run it down to pavement, and I breathed with relief.

"Did you do that, back there?" I finally asked, the question that had been plaguing me since it happened. "Did you send that... cat-demon or whatever it was to take down Todd Tolliver?"

"Cat-demon?" she said lightly. "I don't know what you're talking about."

"There at the last, Todd was heading for the door. Something tripped him. I saw it. I thought it was Isis, but she never moved."

Cat glanced at me, her expression veiled in the darkness. "He fell over his own big feet."

"No. He didn't."

Cat was quiet for a long time. "Well, it wasn't me. I swear. But things do happen, things beyond our ken as the Scots say. Believe what you will, I'm just glad it's over."

The whole thing was beginning to fade in my memory. Suddenly I was no longer sure what I had seen. Maybe he did trip of his own accord. I'd been dazed and missing my glasses. How simple it would have been to make a mistake.

"Did you have any idea it was Todd?" I asked, ready to put the subject of demon-cats away for now.

"The kid from the Pet Pantry?" she noted. "Not at all."

"He seemed to think you'd come into some huge inheritance. Money is a strong motivator," I reflected.

110

"I talked with him a few times at the store. Nothing heavy, and certainly nothing about being a Bremerton-Black. He must have dug up that information on his own. If he'd dug a little farther, he would have found out the truth—that I don't have a bean."

"He really wasn't the most savvy criminal I've come across."

Cat glanced my way. "And you've come across a lot of them?"

"I've met my share," I said ambiguously. More than my share, I reflected, recalling the gem-stealing Badass Brothers, the cat counterfeiter and his serial killer colleague, along with a few more.

"But you're right," Cat agreed. "It struck me from the first, when he called to arrange the meet, that he really didn't know what he was doing. He was totally blindsided when he figured out I hadn't complied with his demands. I was too frightened to recognize it at the time though."

"You said he mentioned a partner."

"Yes, and that scared me too. Todd may not have been the brightest berry on the tree, but what if this partner was smarter, the brains of the operation?"

"Do you think there really was one, or did he make that up to give himself more credibility?"

She considered for a moment. "I don't know. I never saw signs of anyone else. No, I'm almost sure he was working alone."

"And the creepy guys who made a bid for you and Isis? I assume that would be one of the anti-paganists. Someone who wanted to keep you from fulfilling the Winter Solstice ritual."

Cat glanced over at me. "You know about that?"

111

"A little. I have a friend who's a witch."

Cat smiled. "Why am I not surprised."

* * *

We put a hold on further speculation when we hit town and I was occupied with guiding Cat to my house. She maneuvered into the snowy parking strip and shut off the car. Placing her hands in her lap, she sat quietly, as if waiting—or praying.

"Are you and Isis going to be able to do your Solstice thing?" I asked finally.

"Yes, I think so. Will you be going to the fête?"

"No," I sulked. "It's almost midnight—even the diehards will have headed home by now."

She sat for a moment more, then handed me my keys and dug her own out of her pack.

"Do you want to borrow the carrier?" I asked as she sprung the seat forward to collect Isis.

She peered in through the wire grill. "That would be nice. The poor girl's sacked out."

"She's had a traumatic experience." I opened the glove box and pulled out a half-pack of cat treats. "Would she like these?"

Cat examined the package. "Oh, those are her favorites! From the Pet Pantry?"

I got out and came around, holding on to the car for balance. She gathered the carrier, then straightened and faced me.

"Thanks for everything, Lynley. We hardly know each other..."

"That may have been true yesterday, but not so much now."

She sighed. "No doubt. Coming to my rescue was a lot

112

to ask."

She reached forward and gave me a slightly awkward hug. I hugged back. I didn't mention I'd done it for Isis more than for her, but if I had, I think she would have understood.

"Take care," I told her as she slogged to her van.

She gave a wave, got into the vehicle, and with a sputter and a *varoom*, drove away, leaving only a rectangle of pristine pavement to mark her passage.

The porch light went on at Mr. Foley's, and the door opened as the man stared accusingly at me.

I shrugged. "She's gone," I called out.

"About time," he grumbled as he went back inside.

I turned to my house, the big Victorian looming darkly against the slate city sky. It had been daytime when I'd left so the only illumination was a tiny nightlight in the front hallway. In the window, silhouetted against the dull, gold glow, sat Little. The house; the window; the cat—it was the most welcoming sight I'd ever seen.

"Lynley, hey. How'd it go?"

I turned to watch Fredric saunter across the street toward me, so light on his feet the slippery surface never fazed him.

"Fredric, have you been waiting up for me?"

"We caught some snow. I was worried." He peered at the place where Cat's van had been. "But it must have worked out, that money thing. Everybody okay?"

"Yes," I sighed. "It worked out in the end."

"Now that it's over, can you tell me what it was all about, or is it still a big secret?"

"No, I guess not," I said, starting up the front steps, "but let's go inside. I need of a cup of tea."

"You're limping!" Fredric exclaimed.

I turned and looked into the young face, so filled with concern. "That's just another part of the story."

* * *

Fredric made the tea while I sat on the couch, my ankle elevated on the ottoman. Little sat on one side of me and Emilio on the other like ebony bookends. They seemed tense, on guard. Maybe they smelled the fear-sweat on me, or the strange mustiness of the old gas station, or Isis. Or maybe they just knew in their telepathic feline way that I'd gone through a bad time.

In spite of the hour, I called Frannie to let her know I was okay. She had left numerous messages on my voicemail and picked up in one ring.

"Lynley! What happened? You missed the fête. I've been calling..."

"Something came up unexpectedly that took longer than I'd anticipated. I didn't have access to my phone..."

"Lynley, stop!" It was Frannie's turn to interrupt. "Quit being vague and tell me if you're okay."

"I'm fine... now. It's a long story and it's late, but I'll tell you all about it in the morning, okay?"

"That's what you said last time," she reminded me.

I cringed at the recollection. "I know, but this time I'll make good on it. Tomorrow, I promise."

She started to protest but stopped. "Okay. I'll be at the shelter. I start my shift at eight."

"I doubt I'll make it in that early, but I'll catch up with you at some point. How was the fête?"

"It was wonderful! You would have loved it. And everyone missed you. But I'll tell you tomorrow. You sound really tired. Get some rest."

"I will. Thanks, Frannie, for everything."

114

I hung up just as Fredric came with two steaming mugs.

"Moroccan Mint," he announced, "with honey."

I inhaled the heady scent, hot and sweet and restorative, just what I needed to debrief from my encounter. He set the cups on the coffee table, then detoured out toward the front door.

"What are you...?" I began, but when the front hall bloomed with colorful hues, I got it—he'd turned on the Christmas tree lights.

"Now Lynley," he said, swinging his supple frame into a wingback chair and grabbing up his tea, "tell me all."

The young man listened intently, letting me rant and ramble, even whine and moan as needed. By the time I'd finished my tea, the story was done as well.

"So," I wound up, "it wasn't the anti-paganists at all, but Todd Tolliver, from the Pet Pantry."

"I know Todd," said Fredric. "He's at PSU with me."

"Oh?" I remarked with surprise.

"I knew he was having money problems. He told me he'd been living in some vacant building for the past semester to save on rent, but that wasn't enough. He said he might need to drop some classes, or even quit school unless he could get a scholarship or something."

"He must have opted for the *or something*," I harrumphed unsympathetically. "He wasn't a very good criminal though. His heart wasn't in it. His attempt at kidnapping and coercion came straight out of a mystery novel."

"That makes perfect sense," Fredric hooted. "He's a total introvert. He wants to be a writer!"

115

Chapter 14

This holiday, watch out for flowers and plants that are dangerous to your cats, such as poinsettias, mistletoe, holly and other berries, lilies, daffodils, and amaryllis. Also be aware that, plants, flowers, and arrangements may have been treated with dangerous pesticides or preservatives which can cause harm as well. Chocolate, grapes and raisins, onions and garlic, and alcohol are also poisonous to our feline friends.

"...Sleigh bells ring. Are you listening?
   On the street, snow is glistening.
   La da-de-da-da, da-de-da-da,
   Walking in a winter wonderland."

I walked over to the CD player and with a decisive punch of a button, turned it off. Christmas Day had finally arrived, and I still wasn't feeling the spirit. I'd missed the one holiday event I'd been looking forward to, the Starry Night fête, and now was faced with the nightmare of my daughter's holiday soiree. The immaculately decorated condo, the immaculately decorated guests. I could see them now, cocktails in hand, talking about famous artists I'd never heard of and celebrity personalities I couldn't care less about. Little plates of champagne-roasted turkey and almond stuffed olives with Japanese toothpicks. At one point in my life, I could have gotten toasted with the rest of them and convinced myself I fit in, but those days were long past. I loved my daughter, but tonight's party held the potential for all the things I disliked most: insincerity, braggadocio, and drunks.

But enough whining, I told myself sternly. I had to make an appearance. It was expected—required. Seleia would be there, and Fredric; my mother Carol and her roommate Candy, always a fun couple. The food, though nontraditional, would be top notch gourmet. And I could leave after the tiramisu or chocolate ganache tart. Since the soiree started early, I'd have to cut back my time at the shelter, but I could still manage a quiet hour with the cats.

The thing with Cat Black and Isis, Todd Tolliver aka Krampus Boy, and the botched kidnapping at the abandoned gas station had affected me. I'd moved through the last few days in a fog, doing what needed to be done—cleaning house, finishing my holiday shopping, taking care of the cats—but it was all on automatic. I was finding little joy in the joyful season.

In spite of his actions, his violence and threats, I felt sorry for Todd. According to Fredric, he was a gifted writer who wanted nothing more than to finish college and get his degree, then make enough money to buy a little cabin on the coast and settle in to write the great American novel. I sympathized. I understood his reluctance to dive into the impossible debt of today's student loan system. Still, crime wasn't the solution, and now he would pay. Oh well, maybe he could finish out his degree in prison while gaining some new insights for his book.

With or without the Wiccan rituals, winter was now officially upon us. I wondered how Cat's Winter Solstice observance had gone. I had no desire to call and ask, however, the memories still too raw in my mind. If she returned my cat carrier, I'd find out then.

I sipped my coffee and stared out the window. The snow had disappeared and so had the ice, leaving Portland in its normal gray-rain funk. It was still early and I had time for a quick breakfast before heading to the shelter. My party dress was clean and pressed; the presents wrapped. All I would need to do when I came home was paste a smile on my face and go.

I jumped as the phone rang beside me on the table. Looking at the readout, I saw it was Seleia.

"Merry Christmas, darling."

"Merry Christmas, Grandmother. How are you this morning?"

"I'm good," I fudged. "How about you? Were you up at the crack of dawn to see what Santa brought?"

"Oh, Lynley," she said in a very adult fashion, "I'm not a kid anymore."

"I know. I was just joking with you. I do remember those days though. You were very cute in your little nightgown crouching under the Christmas tree. I have pictures to prove it."

"I remember too." She sighed. "It was lovely."

"What about that time we gave you the easel and paints? You were going to be an artist."

She laughed, still a child's laugh I was happy to note. "You gave me a smock, too, just like the ones the Old Masters in the art books wore. I had so much fun painting like a real Master, though I wasn't very good."

"I thought you were excellent," I shot back.

"All I ever painted were cats."

"And what's wrong with that?"

We both laughed, and I felt a bit of Christmas flow into my heart, all warm and sweet like honey-spiced cider.

"So I guess I'll see you tonight," I said, sobering to the

reality of the impending soiree.

"Actually, that's what I'm calling about. Mother has a present for you. Here she is."

"Wait—Seleia..."

Too late. I heard the phone fumble and then the voice of my daughter, so clipped and formal after Seleia's flowing speech.

"Hello, Lynley?"

"Hi, Lisa. What's up?" I asked warily.

"Can't a daughter wish her mother Happy Holidays?" she asked with a slight titter—Lisa's idea of a joke?

"Of course, dear. And Happy Holidays to you too. Are you all set for your festivities tonight?" I asked through gritted teeth.

"Oh, yes, aside from the usual last minute. But that's not why I called." There was a slight pause. "Not really."

I waited. She had something to tell me, and as I ran through the likely prospects, I tried not to fear the worst.

"I want to give you a Christmas present, and I think you'll like it. The family discussed it, and well, we decided that..."

She hesitated, and my anxiety ramped up a notch.

Then, in a jumble of hurried words, she blurted, "You don't need to come to the party tonight."

"Pardon?" I asked without comprehension. I must have heard wrong.

"You certainly can if you want," she quickly continued. "Come, I mean. We'd love to have you. But I know you really don't care for these sorts of events—lots of people, strangers and such... And I wanted to give you the option. If you'd rather do something else... If you think you'd prefer... I just thought you might..."

"Oh, I'm really not any good at this," I heard her say

off to the side.

"Grandmother?" said Seleia, coming back on the line. "What Lisa's trying to tell you is that you can do whatever you want today. That's her gift to you, no obligations. You can come to the soiree if you really want to, but it's up to you. I bet you'd rather skip the crowd and spend Christmas with your shelter cats."

"Well... but I do want to see my family."

"Mother's got that covered too. Tomorrow night we're having a Boxing Day supper for just us—Mum, Dad, Carol and Candy, me and you. It'll be sit-down and casual, and you can visit Solo while you're here. How does that sound?"

I could hardly believe my ears. "Are you saying your mother won't be offended if I don't come to her soiree? That she really, truly won't mind?"

"Really truly." Seleia paused, then said quietly, "She's more sympathetic than you give her credit for, at least sometimes."

"Wow!" was all I could say. "Let me talk to her again."

"Mother," Seleia called.

"Hello, Lynley? Did she explain it to you? It's an odd present, I know..."

"On the contrary, it's extremely thoughtful and I'm deeply touched. I know your party means a lot to you and that you love entertaining, but you're right, it's not as much fun for me."

"I understand, I really do. Christmas is for family, and it shouldn't be a chore. I'm trying to dispense with the obligations and look deeper to the meaning of the season. To tell you the truth, I'm fed up with the commercialism that tells us what we are supposed to do and feel, how we're supposed to observe."

"Good for you! And I'd love to come to Boxing Day dinner tomorrow night."

"Well, that's that then," she said somewhat perfunctorily. "I really must be getting back to my preparations now. A million things to do. You have a wonderful day, and if you change your mind about tonight, you know you're always welcome.

"I love you, Mother," she added in a rare display of emotion.

"I love you too, Lisa. And I love my present! Thank you so much."

"We have a real present for you too of course," she added hastily.

"I'll see you tomorrow, dear. It'll be fun."

I hung up the phone feeling ten times lighter. Now I was free to spend as long as I liked at the shelter with the cats and the interesting assortment of volunteers that chose to donate the holiday to their ongoing care. The small family dinner tomorrow sounded perfect, with quiet conversation and a chance to talk and listen. For the first time, I felt as if I was finally in sync with the spirit of Christmas.

* * *

Three green-aproned volunteers sat on the floor of the colony room surrounded by cats. Blazer, a ten-year-old tuxedo boy who was recovering from a badly broken leg curled up on my lap, and Face-of-Boe, a scrawny, ancient tabby, was draped across my legs. As I'd anticipated, the holiday had brought a diverse collection of folks to the closed shelter. It took a special person to focus their Christmas on cat care.

"I just moved here from Fresno," a girl of college age

explained as she ran a brush through the luxurious coat of a gray Maine coon. "I don't have any family here, so I thought this would be as good a place as any to spend the day. I'm meeting some people later on, and we're going to dinner somewhere, but this..." she gestured around the small room with its fluffy cat beds and tall climbers. "This feels like home."

"I'm glad, Winn," said an older woman, Joan, who, like me, spent a good portion of her retirement time in the voluntary service of FOF. "It's hard moving to a new place, but we're all kindred spirits here. Aren't we, Lynley?"

I nodded. "That we are." I turned to a girl with long brown hair woven into a braid. She was sitting cross-legged in the corner, petting a tiny calico who was slowly and very soberly munching kibble from a bowl. "And what about you, Brianne? What brings you to the shelter today?"

"I had to check on Callie," she replied in a quiet voice. "She's a social eater and won't eat unless someone is with her."

"Not just anyone." Joan smiled. "I've been watching you with her. She's a skittish cat, but she's come to trust you."

Brianne looked down at the brightly colored calico and beamed. "If I could, I'd adopt her myself, but I'm in a temporary living situation right now. Maybe when I find an apartment, if she's still around."

Joan turned to me. "What's your story, Lynley?"

I shrugged. "Nothing special. I can't think of anywhere I'd rather be, besides home with my own cats, which is the sum total of my plan for later tonight."

"No family Christmas?"

"My daughter is giving one of her huge holiday parties with a zillion friends and the cocktails flowing. She loves that sort of thing, but I just can't face it right now." I hesitated. How could I put into words all the details, both tiny and huge, that had brought me to where I was today? "It's been a particularly difficult week," I finally compromised.

Once again I thought back to the kidnapping. I hadn't been hurt, not really—the lump on my head had gone down, the ankle was much better, and the knee merely sported a yellow bruise—but inside, things weren't healing as quickly. I had been made to feel helpless— *again!* I needed to work on that. If I wanted to be strong, I must act strong, get strong. That would be my goal for the coming year: strengthen up! And maybe quit getting myself into so much trouble.

It was a good plan. I didn't feel helpless now—I felt good. I felt at home. I felt... dare I say it? ...Christmassy?

The door opened and closed just as quickly as a middle-aged man, a red and white Santa hat falling to one side of his graying hair, slipped into the room. He sank onto a low stool with an *oof.*

"That knee bothering you again, Don?" Joan greeted her old friend.

"It's better," he sighed. "I think."

Before Don had time to settle, a lean, black shorthair jumped into his lap.

"Hello, Onyx," he said, welcoming the cat as he would any of the humans in the room. Onyx answered with a purr as he curled into a perfect circle.

Don glanced around the small room. "What are you ladies up to on this beautiful Christmas morning?"

"We were telling how we all came to be here today," I

123

said. "Winn just moved to Portland; Brianne's helping Callie eat; I'm here because my family obligation isn't until tomorrow; Joan is always here—sometimes I think she lives here."

Everyone laughed, because it was true.

"What about you, Don?" Joan put out. "Why aren't you home drinking eggnog and assembling impossible toys for those grandkids of yours?"

"I like it here when it's closed and quiet. So different from the hustle of the adoption crowds." A broad smirk crossed the rugged face. "And I'll have you know I've already set up a plush unicorn rocking chair and a three-wheel chopper. Love the kidlets but it's nice to have a little peace before it all gets crazy again tonight." Don ran a hand across Onyx's soft fur, utterly enraptured.

The door cracked again as someone else eased inside. The colony room was plenty big for a dozen cats, but add six people and it was beginning to feel decidedly crowded.

"Hi, Denny," I hailed the handsome young man. "What are you doing here?"

Special Agent Denny Paris was one of Connie Lee's humane investigator partners. He and I were the best of friends, the two of us having been through more trials and tribulations than I could count on one hand. Now, as he stood flattened against the wall, trying—and failing—to keep his tall frame from taking up too much space, I had to smile at his modest manner.

"I'm looking for you," he replied, giving me a cheery grin. "I spotted you through the window. So, what do you think?"

He'd caught me totally off guard. I searched my brain for a clue to what he was talking about and came up empty.

"Um, think about what?"

"Didn't you get my email? I sent it last night."

"Not everybody is glued to their mailbox on Christmas Eve, Denny," Joan gently admonished.

Joan was right: some people had better things to do, such as try to get back to normal after being waylaid and threatened for one's life. In my case, that translated into a cozy TV mystery with my cats, then early to bed. "I'm sorry, I haven't checked since yesterday. What's it about?"

Denny's grin grew wider, as if he had a treat in store. "You know the Cat Summit in Long Beach, mid-January?" he began. "Well, I'm going to be one of the speakers."

"Congratulations..." I began, but he cut me off.

"*And...*" he drawled, "the coordinator told me they could use another person. I immediately thought of you. All expenses paid."

My heart jumped. I'd longed to go to the exclusive cat conference presented by the Humane Society of Long Beach, in Washington, but the registration fee was high. With lodging and meals, no matter how I spun it, I just couldn't fit the extra expense into my budget.

"Really?" I gasped, not believing my good fortune.

"Really," Denny returned. "It's all set. All you have to do is say yes."

"But what would I speak about?"

"Cats, of course."

I wanted to jump up and hug the man for arranging this incredible opportunity, but I had two cats on my lap.

"I'd love to! Yes! I'll need to make some arrangements," I added, trying to remain at least a little pragmatic about the whole thing, "but I'm sure I can work things out."

"Just get back to me in the next couple of days with your photo and bio, and I'll get you on the list."

Denny slipped out again to a chorus of Happy Holidays, leaving me blissfully contemplating the prospect of the Cat Summit.

Aside from the purring of cats, the room had gone quiet, each of us in our own little worlds. Brianne stroked Callie as the small cat methodically crunched her kibble; Winn cleaned silky fur out of her brush and went at the Maine coon for a second run; Joan dangled a ribbon toy for a pair of twin kittens.

I looked at Don in his Santa hat, perfectly contented with Onyx asleep on his lap.

He looked back at me and winked. "Merry Christmas, Lynley."

"Merry Christmas, Don," I replied. And I meant it.

THE END

About the Author

Native Oregonian Mollie Hunt has always had an affinity for cats, so it was a short step for her to become a cat writer. Mollie is the author of **The Crazy Cat Lady Cozy Mystery Series**, featuring Portlander Lynley Cannon, a sixty-something cat shelter volunteer who finds more trouble than a cat in catnip. The third in the series, **Cat's Paw**, was a finalist for the 2016 Mystery & Mayhem Book Award, and the fifth, **Cat Café**, won the World's Best Cat Litter-ary Award in 2019.

Mollie's sci-fantasy, **Cat Summer** (Fire Star Press) is the first in her **Cat Seasons Tetralogy** where cats save the world from an evil older than history—twice! Mollie also published a non-cat mystery, **Placid River Runs Deep**, which delves into murder, obsession, and the challenge of chronic illness in bucolic southwest Washington. Two of her short cat stories have been published in anthologies, one of which, **The Dream Spinner**, won the prestigious CWA Muse Medallion. She has a little book of Cat Poems as well.

Mollie is a member of the Oregon Writers' Colony, Sisters in Crime, Willamette Writers, the Cat Writers' Association, and NIWA. She lives in Portland, Oregon with her husband and a varying number of cats. Like Lynley, she is a grateful shelter volunteer.

A Note from the Author

Thanks so much for reading my cozy cat mystery novella, Cat Noel. I hope you enjoyed it. If you did, please consider leaving reviews on your favorite book and social media sites. Reviews help indie authors such as myself to gain recognition in the literary jungle. Thank you in advance for your consideration.

Cat Noel takes place in the Crazy Cat Lady universe between book six, **Cosmic Cat**, and book seven, **Cat by the Sea** (coming 2020). I suppose you could call it book *six-point-five*. I'm currently working on book eight, **Adventure Cat**, so be assured that Lynley has not cleaned her final litter box or solved her ultimate mystery.

Want more Crazy Cat Lady escapades? Look for the rest of the series for Kindle or in print online at http://www.amazon.com/author/molliehunt.

Cat and poetry lovers, check out **Cat Poems: For the Love of Cats**.
   "This collection of cat poems touches on the joy of becoming acquainted with a newly adopted friend, the heartbreak of saying goodbye to an old one, viewing life through a cat's eyes, and celebrating those who foster and advocate for cats... Every one will touch your heart." —Mochas, Mysteries, and Meows

For those of you who enjoy sci-fantasy, **Cat Summer**, the first book of the Cat Seasons Tetralogy has been released through Fire Star Press.

Mollie Hunt has written a science fiction fantasy that will grab your attention from page one and keep it until the end.
—*Fran Kelso, CWA Author*

Mollie weaves a story that blurs the lines of mythology, spiritualism, mysticism, science and reality that took me into another world. With her use of vivid imagery, I wasn't reading about Lise, the human-cum-feline protagonist and the cats fighting evil, I was in the trenches with them. The continuous struggle of good fighting evil, well, it's frightening—not in the least because so many of the things she's written are real.
—*Ramona D. Marek MS Ed, CWA Author*

Not cat-centric, I've also published a non-cat mystery:

Placid River Runs Deep.
Like stones beneath Placid River, a dark tragedy lurks.

When Ember Mackay learns she has a life-threatening illness, she runs away to her secluded river cabin, but instead of solace, she finds mystery, murder, and a revenge plot that has taken a generation to unfold.

Made in the
USA
Lexington, KY